BENEATH THESE BRANCHES

Haunting Of Darlington House

Kimberly St. Clair

Uncorked Publishing

ISBN: 978-1-7640033-3-9

Cover design by: Art Painter
Library of Congress Control Number: 2018675309
Printed in the United States of America

To those who find beauty in shadows, who seek stories in whispers, and who believe that love endures beyond time. This is for you.

And to my family—this book is for you, with all my love.

"Hell is empty and all the devils are here." — *William Shakespeare, The Tempest*

"Ghosts were created when the first man awoke in the night." — *James M. Barrie*

FOREWORD

In crafting *Beneath These Branches: Haunting of Darlington House*, I found myself drawn to the unsettling whispers of history—those fleeting echoes of lives lost and promises broken.

This novel is not merely a ghost story; it is a reflection on the weight of legacy, the binding nature of blood, and the undying strength of love even in the face of death.

Readers will discover a world where the past refuses to rest and where every choice carries the weight of eternity. I am honored to share this journey with you.

— Kimberly St. Clair

INTRODUCTION

Darlington House stands not just as a structure of stone and timber, but as a testament to time, secrets, and sorrow. This introduction invites readers to step through its creaking doors and into a world where every shadow has a story, every whisper carries a memory, and every heartbeat echoes through generations.

Prepare yourself for a journey through hidden passages and forgotten pacts, where history and the supernatural intertwine. Welcome to *Beneath These Branches: Haunting of Darlington House* — may you find both terror and beauty within its pages.

ALSO BY KIMBERLY ST. CLAIR

We Will No Be Forgotten

Red Snow

Blood And The Devil's Due

PREFACE

Beneath These Branches: Haunting of Darlington House began as a fleeting idea, a whisper from forgotten history. Inspired by ancient curses, lost love, and the chilling weight of unspeakable secrets, this novel explores the fragile boundary between the living and the dead.

Every chapter is steeped in gothic atmosphere, weaving historical details with spectral hauntings. My hope is that readers will feel the same pulse of dread and yearning that guided me through every page. May this story linger in your mind like a restless spirit long after the final word is read.

— Kimberly St. Clair

PROLOGUE

The Darlington estate was never truly silent.

Even on the stillest of nights, when the wind dared not stir the leaves and the moon shied away behind thick clouds, something moved within the bones of the house. The walls, ancient and burdened, seemed to sigh with the weight of secrets long buried, and the shadows stretched too far, lingering where no light could reach.

It was said that the land itself was cursed, its roots soaked in blood and betrayal. The whispers began long before Edward Darlington was born, before Clara Langston's delicate hand traced the lines of forgotten journals, before Silas Boone ever smirked at the unknown. It began with a promise—a pact—sealed in desperation and carried through generations like a haunting melody that could never be silenced.

On the night the pact was made, the air was thick with fear and the scent of damp earth. Thomas Darlington, his hands trembling, stood before the ancient oak, its gnarled branches clawing at the sky like skeletal fingers. Beside him, Isolde Langston's tear-streaked face was pale in the moonlight, her dark eyes wide with dread.

"They will take everything," Thomas whispered, his voice raw with desperation. "The land... our future... our lives."

Isolde's voice was barely audible. "And what will they give in return?"

Thomas's eyes glistened. "Survival."

The ground seemed to pulse beneath their feet, as though the earth itself listened. A figure, cloaked in shadow, stepped forward, its voice a chilling echo. "A life for the land. Blood for blood. Betrayal for prosperity. Do you accept?"

Thomas's whisper was a broken plea. "Yes."

Isolde's cry pierced the night, but it was too late. The pact was sealed.

The tree, once merely ancient, became something more— something terrible. Its roots, unseen, wound their way through the land, binding it to the blood that was spilled. The house that stood upon that soil would never forget. And neither would those who dared to call it home.

Decades later, Edward Darlington would stand beneath that very tree, unaware of the price already paid, unaware of the cost yet to come.

But the branches knew.

And they waited.

Beneath These Branches is a tale of love, sacrifice, and the haunting grip of the past. As Edward, Clara, and Silas uncover the chilling secrets buried within Darlington House, they must face the echoes of those who came before them—and the unrelenting demand of the land that binds them all. This is not just a ghost story; it is a story of the choices we make, the promises we break, and the price we pay when the past refuses to stay buried.

CHAPTER ONE

The road to Darlington House wound through a wilderness long forgotten, a scar carved through tangled underbrush and towering oaks draped in veils of ghostly moss. Evening cloaked the landscape in bruised hues of deep purple and sullen gray, a melancholy sky heavy with the weight of impending night. The air was thick, oppressive in its stillness, steeped in the mingled scents of damp earth, decaying leaves, and the faint, metallic tang of something more ancient—something unsettled. Edward Darlington, seated atop his weary horse, felt every hoofbeat resonate through the brittle ground, a steady drumbeat that echoed in his chest like a funeral march. Fields that had once stretched in orderly rows now lay abandoned, the skeletal remains of cotton and tobacco stalks reaching skyward like bony fingers, clawing at the dusk.

Darlington House revealed itself slowly, a specter rising from the gloom, its once-grand facade a crumbling testament to faded glory. What had once gleamed pristine white now bore streaks of mildew like veins beneath fragile skin, its paint flaking away in brittle ribbons. The great columns that flanked the entrance stood cracked and weary, one leaning precariously, as though bowing beneath the weight of unspeakable history. Hollow windows stared blankly into the encroaching night, dark eyes that reflected nothing, hinting at all that had been lost within its walls. Edward felt the weight of the house's gaze upon him—a silent judgment, a whispered challenge—and for a moment, he hesitated, breath catching in his throat.

Each step toward the house felt deliberate, the crunch of withered grass beneath his boots the only sound in the suffocating silence. The air grew heavier as he approached, laced with the faint scent of rust and dampness, as though the very soil had soaked up centuries of blood and regret. His fingers brushed the banister of the grand staircase, its wood splintered and weary, and the chill that seeped into his skin felt far older than the waning light of day. Inside, shadows clung to every corner, the silence broken only by the faintest creaks of ancient timber settling—or shifting, unseen.

In the parlor, Mary Darlington sat like a relic from another time, her fragile frame barely filling the high-backed chair that once commanded presence. Her eyes, sunken and shadowed, flickered with recognition, with something sharper beneath. "You've come back," she whispered, and the words felt more like an accusation than a welcome. Edward's response caught in his throat, words unspoken pressing against the weight of the house's unseen gaze. As night descended, Edward's footsteps echoed through deserted hallways lined with faded portraits of grim-faced ancestors. The air turned colder still, thick with an unseen presence that clung to the walls, whispering promises of unease.

In the stillness of his childhood room, Edward gazed out at the untamed gardens, the wind carrying the faintest whispers from the tangled branches. His reflection in the window flickered, and for a heartbeat, another face stared back at him, pale and pleading—gone in an instant. Dreams plagued him through the night—visions of murky water closing in, chains dragging across unseen floors, and a woman's voice calling him from the shadows. When he awoke, breathless and shaken, his eyes were drawn to the floor where muddy footprints—impossible footprints—led from the door to his bedside. The door that should have been locked.

But wasn't.

CHAPTER TWO

Morning broke reluctantly over Darlington House, the pale light diffusing through layers of mist that clung stubbornly to the earth, as though even the sun feared casting its gaze upon the forsaken estate. Wisps of fog drifted through the skeletal branches of ancient oaks, their twisted limbs reaching skyward in silent lament. Within the decaying walls of the mansion, the light filtered through cracked shutters, falling in thin, jagged beams that illuminated the dust swirling lazily in the stale air. Each floorboard groaned beneath Edward's measured steps, the sound sharp and hollow in the suffocating stillness. The house felt unnaturally cold, a chill that seeped from the very foundations, as though the bones of the land itself whispered secrets to those willing—or unfortunate enough—to listen.

The fire Edward had kindled in the parlor flickered weakly, its warmth barely reaching the edges of the room. The scent of damp wood mingled with the lingering odor of mildew and the faintest hint of something metallic, an iron tang that settled uncomfortably in the back of his throat. Seated in the high-backed chair, Edward stared into the flames, lost in the labyrinth of his thoughts. The memory of the footprints haunted him more than their physical presence ever had; he had scrubbed them away, but their ghost remained, an unsettling reminder of something unseen. His mind struggled for rationality, blaming fatigue, the unsettling atmosphere, even the capricious nature of old houses, but a shiver ran down his spine, unbidden and unrelenting, as if unseen eyes traced his every movement.

The distant crunch of wheels on gravel broke his reverie, the rhythmic sound growing louder as it approached through the thinning morning fog. Edward rose, tension knotting his shoulders, as he moved to the front steps. His eyes narrowed as the familiar silhouette emerged—broad-shouldered, posture relaxed to the point of insolence. Joseph Darlington had returned. The weight of five years apart, marred by sharp words and severed ties, hung between them like an unspoken curse. Joseph's sharp features were shadowed beneath the brim of his hat, but Edward recognized the restlessness in his brother's eyes, a glint that spoke of roads traveled and regrets buried too shallow.

"Still standing," Joseph drawled, his voice rough as gravel, lips curving into a faint smirk.

"Barely," Edward replied, voice clipped, as if the house itself strained to hear their words.

Inside, the house felt denser, each step an intrusion into its silent gloom. Joseph's gaze lingered on the portrait of Judge Josiah Darlington, his hand almost brushing the frame before falling away. "Old bastard still watching," he muttered.

Mary Darlington's frail voice greeted Joseph with little warmth. "You've come back," she rasped, more observation than welcome.

"Didn't have much choice," Joseph replied, nonchalant, though the air thickened around them.

The afternoon brought Meg, quiet and observant, her presence a balm to the strained atmosphere. Her fingers traced the edges of her sketchbook absently, eyes drifting to the room's dark corners, as if expecting something to emerge from the shadows. The fire crackled, but its light failed to chase away the unsettling gloom.

Night draped the house in a shroud of deeper unease. Edward, drawn by an unseen pull, found himself standing before the locked study. But tonight, the door was ajar. Heart pounding, he pushed it open. The room greeted him with dust-laden shadows and an ominous stillness. The mirror on the desk reflected his pale face—until it didn't. His reflection lingered, twisted into an unfamiliar expression, a heartbeat longer than it should have.

A whisper caressed the silence.

"Edward…"

CHAPTER THREE

Autumn's twilight draped Darlington House in a pall of restless gloom, where even the sun seemed reluctant to touch the cursed earth. The skeletal branches of ancient oaks groaned in the wind, their knotted limbs trembling as if burdened by unseen weight. Within the manor's crumbling walls, Edward Darlington roamed the shadowed halls, each creak of the floorboards echoing like distant cries. Fires lit in the grand parlor sputtered weakly, their warmth unable to pierce the damp chill that clung to the very marrow of the house. Time itself felt fractured, days bleeding into nights, while the land beyond—the withered fields and looming north woods—seemed to inch closer with every passing moment, as though eager to reclaim what had long been abandoned.

Edward's gaze stretched over the decaying fields from the front porch, his hands gripping the wooden railing worn smooth by generations of restless souls. Joseph joined him, the weight of their shared past thick in the stillness. Their exchange was terse, laced with bitterness and unresolved history. As the sun dipped below the horizon, Meg, drawn by an inexplicable pull, climbed the narrow attic stairs. Dust-laden air thickened around her, each step an intrusion into forgotten time. The cracked pane of a solitary window allowed slivers of moonlight to slice through the gloom, illuminating a forgotten trunk marked with the initials E.M. With hesitant fingers, Meg unearthed brittle letters bound by crimson ribbon, their inked confessions whispering of Eleanor Mayfield's unrelenting presence within the house's bones.

As Edward read the fragile letters, their words etched sorrow into his features. Secrets long buried clawed their way to the surface, binding the Darlington legacy tighter to the house's cursed foundation. That night, Edward's fitful sleep was haunted by unseen whispers, the creak of floorboards that betrayed the weight of something unseen. And when his eyes snapped open to the moonlit room, the unmistakable silhouette of a shadow lingered, too tall and too still, dissolving into the darkness as his breath caught in his throat. The echoes of the past had stirred, and Darlington House was far from silent.

CHAPTER FOUR

Morning arrived reluctantly, its wan light smothered by thick clouds that hung low over the land, as though even the sky hesitated to cast its gaze upon Darlington House. The air, heavy with moisture, pressed down upon the crumbling manor, and the earth itself seemed to sigh beneath the weight of something unseen. Edward awoke with a start, the remnants of a forgotten dream clinging to him like cobwebs, the faint echo of a woman's voice whispering through the cavernous silence of the house. His room, shrouded in dim light, bore silent witness to his restless night, and as his gaze fell upon the deep gouges in the wooden floorboards, a chill coiled through him. The scratches, sharp and deliberate, trailed from the wardrobe to the edge of his bed, as if something unseen had clawed its way through the darkness.

Downstairs, the house groaned softly, each creak a mournful lament. Edward found Joseph in the parlor, the morning's gloom mirrored in his weary expression. Their conversation was clipped, filled with tension and unsaid fears, and when Joseph mentioned the footsteps he'd heard in the hall the night before, Edward felt the cold hand of dread tighten its grip around him. As the day stretched on, Meg found herself drawn to the outskirts of the property, her footsteps hesitant yet compelled. The old well, half-forgotten and cloaked in creeping ivy, stood like a sentinel amidst the overgrown grass. She leaned closer, and from its dark depths, a voice—a whisper, unmistakably human—drifted upwards, sending her fleeing back to the house, heart pounding.

Night fell like a shroud, and the house grew restless once more. Edward pored over the letters Meg had discovered, Eleanor Mayfield's frantic words weaving a tapestry of madness and truth. Shadows stretched unnaturally across the walls, and when Edward caught sight of a pale figure standing in the doorway, its eyes hollow and pleading, his heart stilled. He spun around, but the figure was gone. Yet the weight of its presence lingered, and Edward knew that Darlington House was no longer merely haunted—it was awake.

CHAPTER FIVE

Night draped itself over Darlington House like an oppressive shroud, thick and unrelenting, pressing down upon the aging structure until every timber seemed to groan beneath its weight. The wind, which had whispered through the trees all afternoon, now lay still, leaving the grounds in an unnatural silence. Shadows stretched long and jagged across the landscape, the swollen moon casting a sickly yellow glow that transformed every tree and stone into something sinister. The house stood in this eerie stillness like a sentinel, its windows reflecting nothing but darkness, its walls holding in secrets too heavy for the night to carry.

Edward sat hunched in the study, the dim flicker of an oil lamp barely illuminating the worn letters spread before him. Their faded ink whispered secrets of another time, each word soaked in desperation and sorrow. The walls of the room, though unmoving, seemed to close in on him, pressing against his thoughts until they tangled into an indecipherable mess. Eleanor's words haunted him, her frantic scrawl echoing in his mind, intertwining with the memory of the shadow he had seen —or thought he had seen—in the corner of his room the night before. His rational mind clawed for explanations, but none came. The silence in the house was too deliberate, the cold too biting, and the scratches on the floor too fresh.

Then came the sound.

Tap. Tap. Tap.

A muffled knocking, faint but deliberate, resonating through the walls as though something was trapped within them, pleading for release. Edward's breath stilled, every muscle in his body rigid with tension. The sound was distant at first, barely perceptible, but it grew louder, more insistent. He rose slowly, the chair scraping softly against the wooden floor, and approached the wall, each step hesitant. His hand hovered over the faded wallpaper, fingers trembling. The tapping ceased the moment his fingertips brushed the surface, leaving behind a suffocating silence that seemed to throb with unseen menace. Pressing his ear to the wall, Edward strained to listen. There was nothing. Not at first.

Then a whisper, faint but unmistakable.

"Edward."

The voice was close, too close, as though someone stood just behind him, breathing the word into his ear. He spun around, heart hammering violently, but the room was empty. The lamp flickered wildly, casting frantic shadows across the walls before sputtering out, plunging the room into darkness.

Morning came sluggishly, the gray light barely managing to seep through the grime-covered windows. Edward found Joseph in the kitchen, already nursing a glass of whiskey, his face pale and drawn. The silence between them was deafening, filled with the weight of shared fears neither dared voice.

Finally, Joseph broke it, his voice low and edged with something unspoken.

"I heard it again," he muttered, staring into his glass. "The walls."

Edward nodded, the memory of the whisper still clinging to him. Later, Meg sat beneath the gnarled oak at the edge of the property, her pencil sketching without direction. When she glanced down, her drawing showed the house—distorted, shadowed, and in the upper window, a woman's figure, blurred but unmistakable. That night, Edward heard the scratches again, closer now, accompanied by the faintest whisper of bare feet across the floor. The door to the locked study stood ajar, and in the flickering lamplight, Edward saw the crack in the wall—dark, jagged, and growing. From within it came a sound.

Tap. Tap. Tap.

And a voice.

"Let me out."

CHAPTER SIX

Morning broke over Darlington House with the same reluctant lethargy that had become its hallmark, the feeble light struggling to penetrate the thick veil of mist that clung to the grounds. Shadows lingered stubbornly in the corners of the old estate, unwilling to be banished even as the sun's pallid rays stretched across the brittle grass and leafless trees. The wind carried a whisper of something ancient, its chill cutting deeper than the crisp autumn air, carrying the faint scent of damp earth, aged wood, and a metallic tang reminiscent of rusted iron left to bleed beneath endless rains.

Edward stood by the cracked window in his room, his reflection fragmented by the delicate lattice of fractures running across the pane. The man staring back at him was a stranger—his face gaunt, eyes shadowed with sleeplessness, and mouth set in a grim line that betrayed the weight pressing down upon him. His fingers trembled as they grazed the cold glass, a fleeting attempt to reach beyond the boundary between him and the outside world, but all he found was the impassive chill of the windowpane. The whisper from the night before still echoed in his mind, threading through his thoughts like an insidious vine creeping through the cracks of an old wall, unseen but ever-present. "Let me out," it had said, soft yet unmistakable, embedding itself in the marrow of his bones.

Descending the grand staircase, Edward felt the house breathe around him, every creak of the wooden steps a heartbeat in the suffocating silence. The hallway stretched before him, the faded wallpaper curling away from the plaster like desiccated skin peeling from bone. Shadows pooled in the corners, deeper than they should have been, and the portraits that lined the walls seemed more lifelike than before, their painted eyes following him with a keen awareness that sent a shiver down his spine. The faint scent of mildew mingled with something sour, an unfamiliar presence that coiled in the stagnant air.

In the parlor, Joseph sat slumped in a chair, a half-empty glass of whiskey cradled in his hands. His usual bravado was absent, replaced by a weariness that tugged at his features. Edward settled across from him, the tension between them thick and unspoken. Joseph's eyes, dark and hollow, flicked up briefly. "Heard it again," he murmured, voice rough with fatigue. Edward didn't need to ask what. They both knew.

Later, Meg ascended to the attic, the narrow staircase groaning beneath her cautious steps. The attic was a forgotten place, cloaked in dust and shadows, the air sharp and biting despite the warmth outside. She knelt by the old trunk, its surface weathered and scarred, fingers tracing the edges before lifting the lid. Eleanor's letters lay within, their brittle pages whispering secrets of a past unwilling to stay buried. One line struck her like a blow: "The house remembers. It keeps the things we try to forget."

A faint scratching sound interrupted her reverie, soft yet

deliberate, rising from beneath the floorboards. She froze, breath shallow, listening intently. The sound grew louder, closer, until it felt as if it was directly beneath her, clawing its way toward the surface. Heart pounding, Meg fled, the whispers following her down the stairs like a breath against her neck.

That night, Edward roamed the darkened halls, a candle casting flickering shadows that danced along the walls. He paused outside the locked study, hand hovering over the doorknob. The door creaked open, revealing the crack in the wall —jagged and dark, like a wound festering in silence. As he knelt, fingers brushing the rough edges, a whisper floated from the darkness within.

"Help me."

Edward stumbled back, the candle extinguished, leaving him alone in the suffocating blackness with the rhythmic tapping echoing through the walls.

CHAPTER SEVEN

The days bled together in Darlington House, an endless stretch of hours steeped in a twilight gloom that refused to be dispelled. Time itself seemed to warp within its walls, each moment dragging with an oppressive weight that settled in the very bones of those who dared to dwell there. Shadows clung stubbornly to the corners, darker and thicker than they had any right to be, as if the house had absorbed every whisper of light and hope, hoarding them in unseen depths. The thin fingers of dawn, fragile and feeble, scarcely penetrated the grimy windows, casting more shadow than illumination, and Edward felt its insufficiency keenly. Each morning, he awoke with the sensation of having traversed endless, nightmarish landscapes in his dreams—dreams he could never quite recall but felt acutely, their lingering unease coiled tightly around his chest like unseen bindings.

Edward stared at the floor beside his bed, the deep, jagged scratches mocking him with their very existence. They were deeper now, unmistakably fresh, the wood gouged as though something had clawed its way from beneath, desperate and relentless. He wanted to dismiss them, to believe they were the result of restless sleep or his own mind unraveling under the strain, but the weight of the house's oppressive silence made denial impossible. The cold in the room was not the ordinary chill of an autumn morning but something more profound, a biting cold that sank into marrow and lingered, sentient and watchful.

Meg sat in the kitchen, her sketchbook filled with unsettling images—faces with hollow eyes that seemed to scream silently, shadows stretching and distorting as though reaching for unseen prey. Each line on the page bore the frantic energy of a hand guided by something far beyond conscious thought. She stared at the sketches, dread pooling in her stomach. She couldn't remember drawing them, yet here they were, undeniable proof that the house was burrowing into her mind. Joseph, his eyes bloodshot and rimmed with exhaustion, said little as he poured another glass of whiskey, the liquid amber against the bleak morning light. When he finally spoke, his voice was rough and low, barely more than a whisper. "I saw it last night," he said, his gaze distant. Meg didn't ask what—she knew. She had seen it too, though she wished she hadn't.

Edward found himself drawn to the study later that day, unable to resist the pull of the crack that marred the wall. It had widened overnight, dark and jagged, an unnatural wound festering within the plaster. The scent of damp earth and rusted iron filled the room, metallic and cold. As Edward reached out, fingers trembling, he felt an unsettling warmth thrumming beneath the surface—a heartbeat that didn't belong. Then came the voice, faint and mournful. "Help me," it whispered, closer than before, weaving through his thoughts like a forgotten memory brought painfully to the surface.

That night, the scratching returned, louder and more insistent, scraping beneath the floorboards with a desperate rhythm. Edward, Meg, and Joseph gathered in the hallway, their faces pale and drawn. They said nothing, but the house spoke for them now. In the study, Edward pried up the floorboards, heart pounding with every splintering crack of wood. What lay beneath wasn't a body, nor any logical explanation, but a hollow void stretching into impossible darkness, the cold air rising from it sharp with the scent of decay. A shadow shifted just beyond the lantern's reach, and the voice came again, no longer just a whisper but a plea soaked in grief and anger. "Let me out." And in that moment, Edward knew—the house wasn't merely haunted. It was possessed.

CHAPTER EIGHT

The dawn clawed its way through the horizon with a muted, sickly light, its feeble glow casting elongated shadows that stretched like skeletal fingers across the frost-rimmed grounds of Darlington House. The estate loomed in the thin morning mist, its silhouette jagged against the pale sky, each cracked window and splintered beam whispering of stories long buried beneath its foundation. The ancient oaks, their gnarled limbs heavy with draping moss, stood sentinel, their twisted branches seeming to clutch at the house as if trying to drag it down into the cold earth. It was a place of silent screams and restless memories, where time itself felt like an illusion.

Edward sat on the edge of his bed, the weight of the house pressing down on him with a force that felt almost tangible. His reflection in the cracked mirror showed a man eroded by unseen forces, his eyes sunken and haunted, his once-proud frame now a silhouette of uncertainty. The voice beneath the floorboards echoed through his mind, not just a plea for freedom but a command wrapped in cold, unsettling certainty. Let me out. The words lingered like an unspoken curse, each syllable woven into the very fabric of the house.

Downstairs, Meg sat curled in an armchair, her sketchbook clutched tightly, the pages filled with images she could not remember drawing—dark figures with hollow eyes, rooms distorted by unseen forces, chains that seemed to rattle in silent torment. Her fingers trembled as they traced the lines, each stroke a memory stolen from her mind by the house itself. Joseph, his jaw tight and eyes bloodshot from sleepless nights, poured himself another glass of whiskey, the amber liquid offering little comfort. "There's something under this house, Edward," Joseph muttered, his voice hoarse. Edward nodded, the truth of those words etched into his very bones.

As the day waned, Edward found himself drawn to the north woods, where the air was thicker, heavier, laced with the metallic scent of disturbed earth. Each step through the brittle underbrush felt like trespassing. Near an old well, its stones slick with moss, Edward unearthed a bone—small, fragile, unmistakably human. Fear clenched his chest, a silent scream echoing through his mind. That night, the house tightened its grip. The walls felt closer, the air heavier. Edward, Meg, and Joseph gathered in the parlor, the fire casting flickering shadows that danced like malevolent specters. "There's someone under the house," Edward whispered, the certainty in his voice chilling. They pried up the floorboards once more, revealing a hollow space where chains lay rusted and worn, and a skeletal figure bound by time and earth whispered through the silence. "Let us out," the voice called, a symphony of despair and rage that trembled through the very foundation of Darlington House. The house breathed, and they knew—they were no longer its inhabitants. They were its prisoners.

CHAPTER NINE

Night in Darlington House was no longer a quiet surrender to darkness, but a trembling hush filled with unspoken horrors. The walls, like lungs, inhaled and exhaled softly, as though the house itself lived, breathed, and hungered. Shadows swelled and shrank with each flicker of candlelight, while unseen footsteps creaked against the floorboards in slow, deliberate cadence. Edward sat rigid in his bed, his hands gripping the thin blanket as if it could anchor him to sanity. The whispers from beneath the floor had not left him; they clung to his mind, cold tendrils twisting into every thought. "They buried us here." The weight of those words pressed into his chest, heavy as the house itself.

Morning brought no relief. Edward found Joseph in the kitchen, silent and grim, his usual sarcastic bravado stripped away. They exchanged few words, their understanding clear without speech. Outside, Meg stood near the porch, her sketchbook filled with unsettling images she could not remember drawing—fractured landscapes, hollow-eyed figures, and distorted visions of the house itself. When she whispered, "They're under everything," Edward felt the truth coil tight around his throat.

Determined, Edward and Joseph dug in the north field, uncovering not just a grave but a mass burial of bones tangled in rusted chains. Back in the attic, Meg discovered letters penned by Judge Josiah Darlington, revealing the family's dark legacy of blood sacrifices to ensure the land's prosperity. That night, Edward pored over the letters, each word confirming his dread. "The land must be fed." The whispers returned, louder, countless voices pleading, commanding. Edward's breath hitched as shadows crowded around him. "Let us out," they echoed. The house shuddered as if waking fully, its prisoners stirring beneath the earth. Edward knew—there was no escape now.

CHAPTER TEN

The house groaned deeply, a sound that resonated through the floorboards and walls, more than the simple settling of old wood—it was a guttural, living thing, an exhalation from unseen lungs hidden in the darkness beneath. Edward sat hunched at his desk, the letters spread before him like fragments of a nightmare woven into ink and paper. Judge Josiah Darlington's words dripped with cruelty, each sentence a testament to arrogance and control, to the blood sacrifices that had bound the land and the family to unspeakable horrors. The ink might have faded, but the weight of their meaning pressed heavily on Edward's chest, as though the very house conspired to keep him trapped beneath its burden.

He clutched his glass of whiskey tightly, the alcohol doing little to burn away the cold that seeped into his bones. Across the house, Meg paced, her charcoal-stained fingers smudging the edges of frantic sketches that covered her room's floor—visions of twisted figures with hollow eyes, jagged landscapes splitting open to reveal screaming faces, and the house, always the house, looming like a hungry beast. Joseph sat outside on the porch, the bottle in his hand nearly empty, his eyes fixed on the north field where the earth had swallowed their secrets. The trees loomed in stillness, branches contorted into grotesque shapes that clawed at the leaden sky.

Morning was a hollow promise when it arrived. They gathered in the parlor, the weight of unspoken truths dragging the air into a suffocating silence. Edward's voice broke the stillness. "We need to go back." Neither Joseph nor Meg argued. There was nothing left to deny.

The crawlspace beneath the house was colder than memory, the scent of damp earth mingled with the metallic tang of rusted chains and ancient blood. Shadows danced wildly against the stone walls as their lanterns flickered, barely holding the dark at bay. Dirt shifted beneath their feet, disturbed by unseen hands. When they uncovered the rotting wooden door, its surface splintered and hinges rusted, Edward felt the weight of countless unseen eyes watching. The door groaned open, revealing a narrow passage that seemed to pulse with an unnatural heartbeat. The walls, slick with moisture, bore strange markings carved by hands long dead, each symbol a forgotten warning.

The passage led them to a small, circular chamber—a crypt of horrors where bones lay in disarray, chains hung from the walls, and a stone slab in the center held the skeletal remains of someone bound in iron meant to trap, not protect. As Edward reached for the rusted chains, the temperature plummeted, their breath visible in the freezing air. Then, the scream came— piercing and primal, filled with centuries of rage and pain. The lanterns flickered, then died, plunging them into suffocating darkness. And in that blackness, something stirred.

The house was awake.

CHAPTER ELEVEN

The Southern sky stretched pale and endless, its winter light thin and brittle as if it, too, were weary of Darlington House's burden. The estate stood like a forgotten sentinel, its once-proud facade marred by time, weather, and whispers that never faded. Edward leaned against the splintered railing of the sagging porch, his eyes distant as they traced the barren fields stretching endlessly before him. The land, once fertile, now mirrored the house's decay—a silent reflection of loss and rot. The air smelled faintly of ash, of something burnt long ago but never quite extinguished, and Edward's breath misted faintly in the cold.

Behind him, the heavy shuffle of boots announced Joseph's presence. "You've been out here too long," Joseph muttered, lighting a cigarette with fingers that trembled slightly from more than just the cold. Edward didn't respond, his thoughts tangled in the unseen threads that seemed to pull tighter around them each day. Joseph leaned against the post beside him, smoke curling between them. "Thinking's a dangerous game in this place," Joseph added with a dry, humorless chuckle.

Up in the attic, Meg sat in the dusty glow of filtered light, surrounded by her own art. The sketches had grown darker, more frantic, as if her hand had become a conduit for something beyond her understanding. She stared at a half-finished drawing —Darlington House split down the middle, with figures clawing from beneath its foundation. She shivered, not from the cold but from the weight pressing down on her chest. A faint whisper, too soft to catch, made her pause. Was it her imagination? Or something else? She pushed the thought aside, focusing on her charcoal-stained hands.

Days blurred into each other, each filled with Edward's futile attempts to patch the house's decay, Joseph's restless brooding by the north field, and Meg's silent retreat into her art. The house resisted every repair, every effort to bring it back from the brink. Cracks in the walls seemed to deepen overnight, and Edward often woke to find new scratches along the floorboards, their origins unknown. One evening, Edward's fingers traced faint claw marks near his desk, his breath catching as he realized they hadn't been there the night before. The house, it seemed, had secrets it was no longer content to keep hidden.

Late one night, Edward woke to footsteps in the hall— soft, deliberate. He crept to the door, heart pounding, but found the corridor empty, save for the unmistakable scent of damp earth lingering in the still air. When he returned to his room, he noticed new scratches near his bed, faint but fresh. Sleep didn't come again that night, and Edward knew—Darlington House was no longer content to simply haunt them; it was reaching out, pulling them deeper into its grasp.

CHAPTER TWELVE

Time at Darlington House unraveled like an old tapestry, fraying at the edges as days bled into nights without distinction. The house existed outside the normal rules, where hours stretched long and shadows grew bold. Edward often found himself awake before dawn, seated at the worn kitchen table, nursing a cup of coffee that turned cold before it touched his lips. His eyes, sunken with sleeplessness, traced invisible patterns across the cracked tiles. The house's silence wasn't comforting; it was a hollow echo that pressed into his mind, making him question if it was truly silent at all.

Joseph's heavy footsteps broke the fragile quiet one morning, his disheveled appearance a testament to restless nights. His usual bravado was dulled, replaced by a weariness that clung to him. "Ever wonder why we stayed?" Joseph muttered, pouring himself a shot of whatever was left in a dusty bottle. Edward's silence spoke volumes. "Maybe we didn't have anywhere else," Edward finally replied, though his words felt empty. Joseph's bitter laugh lingered in the air like smoke.

Outside, Meg wandered the barren grounds, her sketchbook her only companion. She found herself beneath the old pecan tree, its twisted branches like skeletal fingers against the gray sky. Her pencil moved without thought, drawing an image that made her blood run cold—a crumbling Darlington House with a hollow-eyed figure watching from the doorway. She snapped the book shut, unable to shake the sensation of unseen eyes upon her.

The parlor became their unspoken meeting ground in the afternoons, the flickering firelight casting long shadows. Edward, Joseph, and Meg sat in uneasy silence, the weight of their shared dread pressing down on them. "We don't talk about it," Meg finally whispered, breaking the stillness. Joseph's attempt to dismiss her words was half-hearted. Edward's quiet agreement hung heavier than the smoke curling from the hearth.

That night, Edward woke to the sound of footsteps above him. The attic, where no one should be. The faint light of his lantern revealed footprints in the dust—small, bare, leading nowhere. The weight of the unseen pressed heavier than ever, and Edward knew the house was no longer content to keep its secrets hidden. It wanted to be heard. And it wanted them to listen.

CHAPTER THIRTEEN

The winter air clung to Darlington House with a brittle stillness, sharp enough to cut through layers of fabric and flesh, seeping straight into bone. Morning light crept reluctantly over the horizon, a pale, anemic glow that stretched long, skeletal fingers across the frost-hardened ground. The house itself stood silent, its weathered façade peeling like old skin, the white paint stained and cracked from years of neglect. The chimneys no longer whispered smoke into the sky with the same strength as they once had—just faint tendrils, as if the house were exhaling its final breath with every dawn.

Edward stood in the front hall, his silhouette framed by the tall windows that bled cold light into the room. The dust floated lazily in the weak shafts of morning sun, disturbed only by the faint shift of air when he moved. His reflection glimmered faintly in the cracked glass of the hallway mirror— an image both familiar and strange. His face had grown thinner, the sharpness of his jaw more defined, dark circles carved beneath his eyes like bruises left by sleepless nights. The man in the mirror wasn't the one who'd first crossed the threshold of

Darlington House weeks ago. This man was heavier somehow—not in body, but in soul.

The echoes of last night's footsteps lingered in his mind, carved into memory just as the faint footprints in the attic dust had been etched into the wood. He hadn't mentioned them to Joseph or Meg. Not yet. He wasn't sure if he was protecting them or himself from the questions that would inevitably follow.

He ran a hand through his hair, the cold biting at his fingers, and stepped outside, the porch creaking beneath his weight like an old man groaning in protest. The wind was sharp, carrying the faint, earthy scent of frost-dampened soil, mixed with something older, something he couldn't quite place—iron, perhaps, or decay softened by time. His gaze drifted toward the north field, its barren expanse stretching wide and empty, but never feeling quite as empty as it looked.

There were places on the land where the ground felt different beneath your feet—softer, as if it remembered things the rest of them were trying to forget.

Joseph was already near the tree line when Edward found him, a cigarette dangling from his fingers, its ember flaring briefly as he inhaled. His posture was loose, casual in the way only someone with tightly coiled nerves could pretend to be. The days had carved their marks into Joseph as well—new lines around his eyes, a deeper shadow beneath the easy smirk he sometimes still wore out of habit more than humor.

"You're up early," Edward said, though the remark felt hollow. None of them really slept anymore—not in the way that mattered.

Joseph shrugged, flicking ash to the brittle grass. "Didn't see the point in trying." His eyes, red-rimmed from either exhaustion or whiskey, drifted toward the field. "Something about this place… it feels heavier every day."

Edward didn't respond. He knew exactly what Joseph meant. It wasn't just the weight of the land's history pressing down on them—it was the sense that the house itself was a living thing, breathing in their fears and exhaling silence in return.

After a long pause, Joseph finally added, "Do you ever feel like we're being… watched?"

Edward's heart clenched slightly, but he forced a neutral expression. "Old houses creak. Shadows play tricks."

Joseph huffed out a bitter laugh, shaking his head. "Yeah. Maybe." But his tone suggested he didn't believe it any more than Edward did.

Meg spent her morning in the parlor, sketchbook balanced on her knees, pencil moving with a mind of its own. The fire burned low in the hearth, casting flickering shadows across the faded rug, its warmth unable to fully chase away the chill that settled deep into the corners of the room. The house felt colder, not just from the winter air but from something else —an absence, like warmth had been stripped away deliberately, leaving nothing but hollow space.

She didn't choose what to draw anymore. The pencil seemed to find its own path, guided by something just beneath the surface of her thoughts. She sketched without looking, her eyes distant, her mind half-aware of the world around her. When she finally glanced down, her breath caught.

The page was filled with faces—not detailed portraits, but rough outlines, hollow-eyed figures staring out from windows, lurking in doorways, their features blurred but unmistakably human. Or almost human. She traced one with her fingertip, the paper rough beneath her touch, and felt a cold prickle at the back of her neck as if someone was standing behind her.

She turned sharply.

No one was there.

But the feeling didn't leave.

Later that afternoon, the three of them found themselves in the dining room, a space that had once been grand but now felt like a relic left to gather dust. The long table was scarred with years of use, its surface marred by water stains and faint scratches that told stories no one remembered anymore. The windows were cloudy with grime, muting the winter light into a dim haze that made everything feel just a little less real.

They sat without speaking for a while, the silence between them more comfortable than conversation. It was Joseph who finally broke it.

"There's something wrong with this place," he said quietly, his voice low and matter-of-fact, as if stating the weather.

Edward didn't look up from the cup in his hands. "It's old. Houses like this have... creaks and drafts. That's all."

Meg snorted softly, not with humor but with disbelief. "Is that what you really think?" She leaned forward, her eyes sharp and clear for the first time in days. "Or is that what you're telling yourself because the truth is worse?"

Edward's jaw tightened, but he said nothing.

Joseph tapped ash into an empty saucer, his gaze distant.

"It's not just the house." He glanced toward the windows, his expression darkening. "It's the land. It's like the ground remembers things we've tried to forget."

The words settled like dust, impossible to sweep away.

That night, Edward found himself awake again, staring at the ceiling, the faint sounds of the house filling the silence —the creak of wood shifting, the groan of old pipes, the distant whisper of wind slipping through cracked shutters. But there was something else beneath it all—something quieter, almost imperceptible.

He rose, drawn by a feeling he couldn't name, and found himself back in the hallway outside Meg's room. The door was slightly ajar. Inside, Meg was asleep, her sketchbook resting on her chest, her face peaceful in a way that felt fragile, as if any sudden movement would shatter the illusion.

Edward's gaze drifted to the pages of the sketchbook. He stepped closer, careful not to wake her, and gently lifted the cover.

The drawings were darker now—not just in content, but in tone. Heavy pencil strokes carved deep into the paper, shadows layered upon shadows. Figures stood in the corners of rooms, their faces hidden, their bodies twisted unnaturally.

And there, on the final page, was a drawing of Edward.

But it wasn't just him.

Standing behind him, drawn in faint, almost invisible lines, was a figure—**tall, dark, faceless—**its hands reaching toward his shoulders.

Edward's breath caught, his heart pounding in his chest. He closed the sketchbook quietly, his hands trembling slightly, and backed out of the room.

In the hallway, he paused, his ears straining in the silence.

From somewhere deep within the house, he thought he heard it—a faint whisper.

Not words. Just... breath.

CHAPTER FOURTEEN

The morning light crept into Darlington House with the hesitance of an unwelcome guest, filtering through the warped shutters in thin, fractured ribbons. It did little to chase away the shadows that seemed stitched into the very walls, clinging to the corners as if the darkness itself had roots buried deep beneath the floorboards. The house was quiet, but not with the peaceful stillness that comes from rest. It was the kind of quiet that listened, that waited, stretching itself thin between the spaces where people lived and breathed.

Edward sat at the small desk in his room, the faint scratch of his pen against paper the only sound in the fragile morning stillness. The letter he was writing was addressed to no one in particular, the ink bleeding slightly into the brittle paper, its edges curled from the damp that never seemed to leave the house entirely. The words came slowly, hesitant, as if each one was a weight he wasn't sure he wanted to carry. They weren't meant to be sent—just a way to anchor himself in the present, to feel like he still existed beyond the walls that seemed to be closing in a little more each day.

Dear Father, he wrote, though the word felt foreign,

hollow. His hand hovered above the page, the ink drying mid-thought. There was nothing to say that hadn't already been buried alongside the man who'd left them nothing but debts and a crumbling house full of ghosts—whether real or imagined. He set the pen down, his fingers lingering on the cool metal as if it might tether him to something solid.

The faint creak of floorboards from the hallway pulled him from his thoughts. Not the sharp, deliberate sound of footsteps—but softer, like someone—or something—shifting their weight just out of sight. He didn't move, didn't breathe for a moment, his heart ticking louder than the old clock downstairs. But the sound faded, swallowed by the familiar groan of the house settling—or pretending to.

Downstairs, Meg sat curled in the faded armchair near the parlor window, her sketchbook open but untouched. The pencil rested loosely between her fingers, the pages filled with drawings that felt less like art and more like confessions. She stared out across the yard, the frost-tipped grass brittle under the weak morning sun. The north field stretched beyond the trees, a dark patch of earth that never seemed to thaw completely, no matter how bright the day.

She'd stopped trying to explain the things she felt when she looked at that field. There were no words that didn't sound foolish the moment they left her mouth. But it was there—an ache, a pull, as if the ground itself remembered things no one else did. Sometimes she thought she could hear it—not voices, not exactly—just the faint hum of something alive beneath the soil.

Joseph's footsteps broke the silence as he entered the room, his presence filling the space like smoke—hard to ignore, even when uninvited. His shirt was wrinkled, sleeves rolled to the elbows, exposing the faded ink of an old scar along his forearm, a faint reminder of days spent fighting battles outside the walls of Darlington House. But this house didn't care about old wounds. It had a way of making new ones.

"You haven't been outside today," he remarked, dropping onto the couch with the kind of careless grace that masked how tightly wound he really was.

Meg didn't look at him. "There's nothing out there I need to see."

Joseph scoffed, leaning back with his arms draped over the worn cushions. "Could say the same for in here."

Silence settled between them, not heavy but familiar, like an old coat you put on without thinking. They'd grown accustomed to it—the space filled more with what wasn't said than what was.

After a while, Joseph broke it again, his voice softer this time. "You ever feel like the house is...watching us?"

Meg finally glanced at him, her expression unreadable. "It's not the house."

She didn't elaborate. She didn't need to.

Later that afternoon, Edward found himself drawn outside, his coat pulled tight against the cold wind that swept across the barren yard. The porch steps groaned beneath his weight, brittle from years of neglect and too many harsh winters. His boots crunched over the frost-hardened dirt as he made his way toward the edge of the north field, where the ground seemed to hum beneath his feet, faint but persistent, like the low thrum of a heartbeat buried deep below.

He stood there for a long time, his gaze fixed on nothing in particular, the emptiness of the field both comforting and suffocating. The sky above was a pale smear of gray, clouds stretched thin like fabric worn down by too much use. The wind carried the faint scent of something metallic, sharp and out of place, like rust left to fester under layers of damp earth.

Edward crouched, running his fingers through the brittle grass, the soil beneath colder than it should have been. His hand brushed against something solid—a shard of old glass, smooth on one side, jagged on the other, its surface cloudy with age. He turned it over in his palm, feeling the weight of it, though it was light as a feather.

Something about it felt wrong.

Not because it was there, but because it felt like it had been waiting for him to find it.

That evening, the house felt heavier, the air thick with the faint scent of wood smoke and something less familiar—dampness, decay, like wet stone hidden beneath layers of plaster. The fire crackled weakly in the hearth, casting long shadows that seemed to move even when nothing else did.

Edward sat at the kitchen table, his hands wrapped around a mug of tea gone cold, staring at the shard of glass he'd found. Meg entered quietly, her eyes drifting to the object in his hand before meeting his gaze.

"Where'd you find that?" she asked softly.

"The field."

She didn't respond, just pulled out a chair and sat across from him, her fingers tracing patterns in the thin layer of dust on the table.

Joseph joined them moments later, dropping into the remaining chair with a sigh that sounded heavier than the day itself. He glanced at the shard, then at his siblings, his expression unreadable.

"Maybe we should leave," he said suddenly, the words sharp in the quiet room.

Edward's jaw tightened. "And go where?"

Joseph shrugged. "Anywhere but here."

Meg's fingers stilled, her gaze distant. "We can leave the house. But it won't leave us."

The words settled like ash, soft but impossible to ignore.

Edward didn't sleep that night.

None of them did.

CHAPTER FIFTEEN

T he wind howled across the barren fields of Darlington House like a wounded thing, rattling the warped shutters and sliding through the cracks in the weathered walls. It carried with it the faint scent of ash and earth, mingling with the metallic tang of rusted iron hidden beneath the soil. The sky above was a bruised gray, heavy with clouds that threatened snow but never delivered, leaving the air thick with a cold that felt less like weather and more like something older, something buried.

Edward stood by the parlor window, the glass cold against his fingertips as he traced the faint lines etched into its surface—cracks like spiderwebs, thin but spreading, as if the house itself was fracturing slowly, piece by fragile piece. His reflection stared back at him, distorted by the imperfections in the glass, a ghost of the man he'd been when they first arrived. His face was thinner now, his eyes shadowed with sleeplessness, the lines around his mouth etched deeper from days filled with silence and nights filled with things he couldn't explain.

He watched the north field, its dark soil streaked with patches of frost, the ground uneven in places where the earth seemed to have shifted. There were no clear markers, no signs of disturbance that would draw attention from someone unfamiliar with the land—but Edward knew every inch of it. He could feel the difference, not just beneath his feet but beneath his skin. The ground wasn't just shifting; it was settling, like something beneath it was trying to rise.

Joseph entered the room without announcement, his footsteps heavy on the worn wooden floor. He carried a bottle loosely in one hand, the glass catching the weak afternoon light. His presence filled the space like smoke—dense, hard to ignore. He didn't say anything at first, just moved to the fireplace, poking at the embers with the iron poker as if the fire could answer questions neither of them dared to ask.

"You're up early," Edward muttered, his voice rough from disuse.

Joseph snorted, not looking up. "Didn't sleep."

Neither of them had.

Silence stretched between them, thick with the weight of things unsaid. Edward didn't ask about the nightmares. He didn't need to. The dark circles under Joseph's eyes spoke louder than words.

After a while, Joseph broke the silence. "I heard something last night." His voice was low, casual, as if they were discussing the weather.

Edward's fingers tightened against the window frame. "The house always makes noise."

Joseph turned, his expression unreadable. "It wasn't the house."

Meg sat on the steps leading to the attic, her sketchbook

balanced on her knees, the pencil moving in quick, sharp strokes. She didn't look at the page as she drew—didn't need to. The lines seemed to guide themselves, her hand nothing more than a vessel for whatever the house wanted to say. She'd stopped fighting it days ago. There was no point.

When she finally glanced down, her breath caught.

The page was filled with dark shapes—figures standing in doorways, watching from windows, their features blurred, indistinct. But it was the center of the drawing that made her heart pound: a staircase, much like the one she sat on now, leading downward into darkness. At the base of the stairs, something waited.

She slammed the sketchbook shut, her hands trembling slightly. But the feeling didn't fade. The sense of being watched clung to her like dust, settling into the spaces between her ribs.

That evening, the three of them gathered in the dining room, the table between them scarred and worn from generations of use. The oil lamp flickered weakly, casting shadows that danced along the cracked plaster walls. The house groaned softly in the background, the sound no longer something they could ignore.

Joseph poured himself a drink, the liquid amber in the dim light. "This place is falling apart," he muttered, though they all knew he wasn't talking about the house.

Edward stared at the grain of the wood beneath his fingers. "It was broken long before we got here."

Meg's gaze drifted between her brothers, her expression unreadable. "It's not just the house," she said softly. "It's what's inside it."

Joseph laughed, but there was no humor in it. "What, like ghosts?"

Meg didn't flinch. "Not ghosts. Something else."

The words settled over them like ash, impossible to ignore.

That night, Edward found himself awake again, his heart pounding for reasons he couldn't name. The house was too quiet, the kind of silence that felt deliberate. He rose from his bed, the floorboards cold beneath his bare feet, and made his way down the hall.

The door to the attic was slightly ajar.

His hand hovered over the doorknob, his pulse a steady drumbeat in his ears. He pushed the door open slowly, the hinges groaning in protest. The attic was dark, the faint moonlight casting long shadows across the dusty floor.

Something moved.

Just a flicker in the corner of his eye.

He turned sharply, his breath caught in his throat. But there was nothing there.

Just dust. And silence.

But when he looked down, he saw it—footprints in the dust, leading deeper into the attic, where the shadows grew darker.

Edward didn't sleep that night.

CHAPTER SIXTEEN

T he cold had settled into Darlington House like an uninvited guest that refused to leave, creeping into every crack and hollow, pressing itself against the thin windowpanes, seeping through the walls until it wasn't just the air that felt cold—but the very bones of the place. Morning arrived reluctantly, the light gray and indifferent, casting long shadows that stretched across the warped floorboards like fingers reaching for something just out of sight.

Edward sat at the small wooden table near the kitchen, his hands wrapped around a chipped mug of lukewarm coffee, though he wasn't drinking it. The steam had long since faded, leaving only the bitter scent lingering in the stale air. His eyes were hollow, dark circles etched deep beneath them, evidence of another night spent chasing sleep that never came. The house had grown quieter over the past few days—not the comforting quiet of solitude, but the kind that listened, the kind that held its breath, waiting.

He glanced toward the cracked glass of the small window above the sink, his reflection faint, distorted. The frost outside had etched delicate patterns along the edges, like veins, spiderwebbing outward. Beyond that, the north field sat empty, barren and brittle under a sky that never seemed to brighten fully. But Edward didn't look at the field for long anymore. There was something unsettling about the way the ground seemed to shift when you weren't watching, as if the earth itself was restless beneath its frozen surface.

Joseph entered the kitchen with his usual careless shuffle, his shirt wrinkled, sleeves pushed up past his elbows, revealing the faint scars that crisscrossed his forearms like old maps leading nowhere. His expression was unreadable, his jaw tight with the kind of tension he didn't bother hiding anymore. Without a word, he grabbed a glass from the shelf, filled it with whatever was left in the bottle on the counter, and slumped into the chair across from Edward.

They sat in silence for a while, the weight of unspoken words filling the room like smoke.

Finally, Joseph broke it. "I saw something last night." His voice was low, casual, as if they were talking about the weather.

Edward didn't look at him. "We all see things in this house."

Joseph's jaw clenched slightly. "Not like this."

Edward finally glanced up, his eyes sharp despite the exhaustion etched into his face. "What did you see?"

Joseph hesitated, his fingers tightening around the glass. "I thought it was you. Standing in the hall. But when I called out, you didn't answer. You just...stood there. Then you were gone."

Edward's stomach twisted, but his face remained impassive. "It wasn't me."

Joseph didn't argue. He didn't have to.

Meg spent most of her day in the attic, her sketchbook balanced on her knees, though she hadn't drawn anything in hours. The pages were filled with dark, frantic lines—faces that blurred at the edges, figures standing just beyond doorways, their features obscured by shadow. She'd stopped trying to make sense of them. They weren't drawings. They were something else. Something the house needed her to see.

She stared out the small attic window, her breath fogging the glass. The view was limited, framed by the twisted branches of an old oak tree whose limbs stretched across the roof like veins pressed against thin skin. The wind rattled the glass softly, a faint, rhythmic tapping that seemed almost deliberate.

She closed the sketchbook abruptly, unable to shake the feeling that if she kept drawing, she'd see something she wasn't ready to face.

That evening, the three of them gathered in the parlor, the fire burning low, casting flickering shadows that danced across the cracked plaster walls. The silence between them felt heavier than usual, as if the house itself was pressing down on them. Edward stared into the flames, his thoughts tangled with memories that didn't feel like his own anymore. Joseph nursed a glass of whiskey, his fingers tapping against the rim with a restless rhythm. Meg sat curled in the armchair, her knees drawn to her chest, her sketchbook resting beside her like an unspoken threat.

Finally, Edward spoke. "Do you ever feel like... this house is watching us?"

Joseph let out a sharp breath, half-laugh, half-scoff. "Feels more like it's waiting."

Meg's gaze drifted to the dark corners of the room, her

voice barely above a whisper. "Maybe it's both."

They didn't talk much after that.

Later that night, Edward woke with a start, his heart pounding, though he couldn't remember the dream that had pulled him from sleep. The room was dark, the faint glow of the dying fire casting long, thin shadows across the walls. He sat up slowly, his breath visible in the cold air, and listened.

The house was silent.

But not empty.

He rose, the floorboards cold beneath his feet, and made his way down the hall. The door to the attic was slightly ajar.

His hand hovered over the doorknob, hesitation thick in his chest. He pushed the door open slowly, the hinges groaning softly. The attic was dark, the faint moonlight casting thin lines of silver across the dusty floorboards.

And there, just beyond the reach of the light, something moved.

A shadow. Shifting. Watching.

Edward didn't breathe. Didn't blink.

But when he stepped forward—it was gone.

CHAPTER

SEVENTEEN

The morning light crept reluctantly into Darlington House, casting thin ribbons of pale gray across the floorboards, barely strong enough to chase away the shadows that clung stubbornly to the corners. The cold was sharper today, not just the lingering bite of winter seeping through the cracks in the walls, but something deeper—a chill that felt as though it was rising from beneath the floor, threading through the house like veins of frost etched into old glass. The house itself seemed to shrink against it, the walls groaning softly, as if protesting a weight they could no longer bear.

Edward sat at the kitchen table, his hands wrapped around a chipped mug of coffee gone cold long before he'd even thought to drink it. The lines etched into his face seemed deeper in the fragile morning light, shadows pooled beneath his hollow eyes, dark and restless. He stared through the cracked window above the sink, out toward the north field, where the ground stretched wide and barren under the bruised sky, the soil darker than it had any right to be. The land had always been difficult —unforgiving in the way the South could be—but lately, it felt different. It wasn't just empty; it felt vacant, as if something had been taken from it, something essential, leaving only a hollow shell behind.

He didn't hear Joseph enter until the floorboards creaked under his weight, his footsteps heavier than usual, carrying the residue of another sleepless night. Joseph moved with the kind of restless energy that had nowhere to go, his shirt rumpled, sleeves pushed up past his elbows, exposing the faint lines of old scars that crisscrossed his forearms like remnants of stories he never told. He poured himself a glass of whatever was left in the dusty bottle on the counter, his fingers steady even as his eyes betrayed the exhaustion buried deep beneath.

"You didn't sleep," Edward observed quietly, though it wasn't a question.

Joseph snorted, the sound dry and humorless. "Did you?"

Edward didn't answer.

They sat in silence, the only sound the faint ticking of the old clock in the hall, though Edward couldn't remember the last time he'd wound it. The air between them was thick with the weight of unspoken things, words that had been left unsaid for too long, festering like wounds that refused to heal.

After a while, Joseph broke the silence. "I heard it again last night."

Edward's jaw tightened, his gaze fixed on the window. "The house creaks. Old wood shifts with the cold."

Joseph's laugh was sharp, brittle around the edges. "It

wasn't the house."

Edward didn't argue, because deep down, he knew Joseph was right.

Meg spent most of the morning in the attic, her sketchbook open on her lap, though she hadn't drawn anything in hours. The pages were filled with dark, frantic lines—faces half-formed, eyes hollow, shadows that seemed to stretch beyond the edges of the paper. She traced the lines with her fingers, the graphite smudging against her skin, leaving faint marks like bruises.

The attic was colder than the rest of the house, the air thinner somehow, as if the space itself was trying to collapse inward. She sat by the small, dusty window, her breath fogging the glass as she stared out at the skeletal branches of the old oak tree just beyond the roofline. The wind rattled the windowpane softly, a faint, rhythmic tapping that seemed almost deliberate, like fingers drumming against glass.

She didn't flinch when the door creaked open behind her.

Edward's shadow stretched across the floorboards, long and thin in the dim light. He didn't speak at first, just stood there, his presence filling the space like the house had grown too small for the both of them.

"You've been quiet," he said finally, his voice low, rough from disuse.

Meg didn't look at him. "There's not much to say."

Edward stepped further into the room, his gaze drifting over the scattered sketches, the faint tremor in his hand betraying the calm he tried to wear like armor. "You've been drawing the same thing over and over."

Meg's fingers tightened around the pencil. "It's not the same."

Edward crouched beside her, picking up one of the sketches. It was another doorway—their doorway—but the shadows beneath it were wrong, stretched too far, too dark, as if something was pressing against it from the other side.

"What do you see when you draw these?" he asked quietly.

Meg's voice was barely a whisper. "Not what's there. What's trying to be."

Edward didn't know how to respond to that.

Later that afternoon, the three of them found themselves in the parlor, the fire burning low, casting flickering shadows that seemed to move even when nothing else did. The house groaned softly around them, the faint sound of the wind slipping through the cracks in the walls like a whisper too faint to catch.

Joseph sat near the hearth, his glass dangling loosely from his fingers, staring into the flames as if they held answers he couldn't find anywhere else. Edward stood by the window, his arms crossed tightly over his chest, his gaze distant. Meg curled into the armchair, her knees drawn to her chest, the sketchbook resting beside her like an unwelcome guest.

The silence stretched thin between them until Joseph finally broke it, his voice rough. "What if we left?"

Edward didn't turn around. "And go where?"

Joseph's jaw tightened. "Anywhere but here."

Meg's voice was soft, but it carried. "It wouldn't matter."

Joseph shot her a sharp look. "Why?"

She met his gaze, her expression unreadable. "Because it's not the house. It's us."

The words lingered long after the fire burned low.

That night, Edward woke to the faint sound of whispers —soft, just beyond hearing, like voices carried on the wind. He sat up slowly, his heart pounding, his breath visible in the cold air. The room was dark, shadows pooled in the corners like something spilled and never cleaned up.

He rose from the bed, his footsteps quiet against the creaking floorboards as he made his way down the hall. The door to the attic was ajar again, just slightly, as if it had been left that way on purpose.

His hand hesitated on the knob. Then he pushed it open.

The attic was empty.

But when he turned to leave, he saw it—a faint outline in the dust on the floor.

Footprints.

Leading toward the far corner.

And stopping there.

But nothing was there.

Nothing he could see.

CHAPTER EIGHTEEN

The sky stretched low and gray over Darlington House, pressing down like a weight too heavy for the brittle landscape to carry. The thin winter light filtered through the fractured glass of the windows, its weak glow casting pale streaks across the warped floorboards, highlighting every imperfection, every hairline crack that splintered through the old wood like veins beneath skin. The house seemed smaller with each passing day, as if the walls were inching closer together, folding inward, swallowing the spaces where warmth and laughter might have once existed. But there was no warmth left in Darlington House—only the brittle chill of history lingering like a ghost that refused to be forgotten.

Edward sat at the long dining table, his fingers tracing the faint grooves etched into the surface—marks left behind by generations long gone, their presence carved deeper into the wood than any memory he could summon. The room smelled faintly of cold ash and dust, layered with that other scent he couldn't name—something metallic, sharp, like rust clinging to the edges of forgotten nails buried deep within the walls. His coffee had gone cold again, untouched, the dark liquid reflecting the faint light like a murky mirror.

The house was too quiet. Not the comforting stillness of solitude, but the oppressive kind, the kind that pressed against your ears and made you aware of every heartbeat, every shallow breath. Even the usual creaks and groans seemed subdued, as if the house itself was holding its breath, waiting.

Joseph entered without a word, his footsteps heavy on the uneven floorboards, each step punctuating the silence like a metronome counting down to something they couldn't see. He moved with the kind of restless energy that suggested he'd rather be anywhere else but had nowhere left to go. His face was drawn, the stubble along his jaw darker, more pronounced, and his eyes carried the weight of too many sleepless nights, shadows etched beneath them like bruises left by dreams he couldn't escape.

He poured himself a drink—something dark and bitter, the kind of drink that burned more than it soothed—and slumped into the chair across from Edward. For a long time, neither of them spoke. Words felt useless, brittle things that crumbled under the weight of the house's silence.

Finally, Joseph broke the quiet, his voice rough from disuse. "I heard it again last night."

Edward didn't ask what. He already knew.

Joseph stared into his glass, swirling the contents absently. "It's getting louder."

Edward's fingers stilled against the table, his jaw tightening slightly. "It's just the house."

Joseph's laugh was dry, brittle around the edges. "Yeah. Just the house." But his tone was hollow, filled with the kind of disbelief that didn't need to be spoken aloud.

Meg spent the morning outside, wrapped in her worn coat, her breath visible in the sharp winter air. The sky was the color of old bone, stretched thin over the barren landscape. She moved slowly, her footsteps crunching softly over the frost-hardened ground, the brittle grass whispering beneath her boots. The land felt different out here—emptier, but not in a way that suggested absence. It was the kind of emptiness that felt deliberate, like something had been scraped clean, leaving only the hollow shell behind.

She found herself standing near the edge of the north field, her gaze fixed on the dark soil that stretched beyond the crooked fence line. The ground seemed to ripple faintly in the cold light, not with movement, but with memory—layers upon layers of things buried just beneath the surface, too deep to see but too loud to ignore.

Meg knelt, her fingers brushing over the brittle grass, feeling the cold seep into her skin, sharp and immediate. She pressed her palm flat against the earth, her eyes drifting closed for just a moment. The ground was colder than it should have been, as if the frost hadn't just settled on the surface but had seeped deep, coiling around the bones of the land itself.

When she opened her eyes, she wasn't sure what she'd expected to see. But there, in the faintest outline, were marks in the dirt—subtle, almost imperceptible, like something had been dragged or had clawed its way through the frost-softened soil.

She didn't call for Edward or Joseph. She just stood, brushing the dirt from her hands, and walked back toward the house, the chill following her like a shadow.

That evening, the three of them sat in the parlor, the

fire burning low, casting long shadows that seemed to stretch further than they should, bending around corners, curling into spaces that should have been too small to hold them. The room felt heavier than usual, the air thick with the faint scent of smoke and something else—something sour, like old wood left to rot beneath standing water.

Edward stared into the flames, the flickering light reflecting in his eyes, making them look sharper, more hollow. Joseph sat with his glass dangling from his fingers, the contents forgotten, his gaze distant, fixed on a point just beyond the edge of the hearth. Meg sat near the window, her knees drawn to her chest, her sketchbook resting beside her, closed but still heavy with the weight of things she'd drawn without understanding why.

The silence stretched thin between them, filled only with the soft crackle of the fire and the faint groan of the house settling—or pretending to.

Edward spoke first, his voice low, more to the fire than to anyone else. "I found footprints in the attic."

Joseph didn't react at first, just took a slow sip from his glass before setting it down with a soft clink. "Yours?"

Edward shook his head. "No."

Meg's fingers tightened around her knees, her gaze still fixed on the frost-streaked window. "They're not ours."

Joseph snorted, but the sound lacked any real humor. "Great. So we've got ghosts now?"

Edward didn't answer. He didn't need to.

The fire hissed softly, as if in response.

Later that night, Edward woke again, his heart pounding, his breath sharp in the cold air. The house was silent, but not empty. He could feel it—the same way you feel the presence of someone standing just behind you, even when you know you're alone.

He rose slowly, his footsteps soft against the creaking floorboards, and made his way down the hall. The door to the attic was ajar again, just enough to see the darkness pressing against the edges of the dim light spilling from the hallway.

His hand hesitated on the doorknob. Then he pushed it open.

The attic was cold, the air thinner somehow, harder to breathe. The moonlight cast pale streaks across the dusty floorboards, and there, faint but unmistakable, were the footprints—leading deeper into the dark, stopping near the far wall.

Edward followed them, his breath visible in the cold, his heart a steady drumbeat in his chest.

When he reached the end of the trail, he stopped.

The footprints ended at the wall.

But the wall was wrong.

The plaster was cracked, the faint outline of something hidden beneath it just visible in the moonlight—an outline of a door that wasn't supposed to be there.

Edward didn't sleep the rest of the night.

CHAPTER NINETEEN

The morning light crept into Darlington House with all the warmth of a dying breath, fragile and thin, casting faint streaks across the dust-choked air. It pooled weakly in corners where the darkness seemed to linger just a moment longer than it should have, unwilling to retreat completely. The house groaned softly, the timbers settling—or so Edward told himself—though the sound felt more like an exhale, like something beneath the floorboards had been holding its breath all night.

Edward hadn't slept. The memory of the footprints and the faint outline of the hidden door in the attic pressed against his mind like fingers against glass—unseen but undeniable. His thoughts were brittle, frayed at the edges, unraveling with every hour he spent pacing the hallways, the weight of the house sitting heavy on his chest. The door wasn't supposed to be there. But it was. And now he couldn't stop thinking about what might be behind it.

The kitchen felt colder than usual as he stood by the cracked window, the frost outside painting delicate veins across the glass, reflecting the tangled mess of thoughts inside his head. The house was always cold now, the kind of cold that settled deep into the bones, indifferent to fires or blankets. He wrapped his hands around a mug of coffee, not for warmth—there was none to be found—but for something to anchor him, something to hold onto.

Joseph entered without a word, his footsteps heavy, dragging slightly as if the weight of the house had settled into his limbs too. His eyes were bloodshot, the dark shadows beneath them carved deeper than usual. He poured himself a drink—something stronger than coffee—and leaned against the counter, his posture loose but tense in the way that meant he was trying not to think about something he couldn't ignore.

Edward didn't bother with small talk. "There's a door in the attic."

Joseph paused mid-sip, lowering the glass slowly. "A door?"

Edward nodded, his fingers tightening around the mug. "It's hidden. Behind the wall. I saw it last night."

Joseph didn't laugh, didn't scoff. He just stared at Edward for a long moment, his jaw tight. "And you didn't open it?"

Edward shook his head. "Didn't seem like the right time."

Joseph huffed out a breath, something between a laugh and a sigh. "When is the right time to open a door that's not supposed to be there?"

Neither of them answered.

Meg found them an hour later, sitting in the parlor, the tension between them thick enough to choke on. She noticed it immediately, the way Edward's jaw was clenched, the way Joseph's fingers tapped absently against his glass, a restless rhythm that never seemed to settle.

"What's wrong?" she asked, her voice soft but sharp enough to cut through the quiet.

Edward didn't look at her. "There's a door in the attic."

Meg didn't react the way he expected. No surprise. No skepticism. Just a slow, shallow breath, as if she'd known all along.

"I've seen it," she whispered. "In my drawings."

Joseph rubbed a hand over his face, his fingers lingering at his temples. "Of course you have."

They sat in silence for a while after that, the house groaning softly around them, the walls pressing inward, listening.

They climbed the attic stairs together later that afternoon, the faint light from the narrow window casting long shadows that stretched ahead of them like brittle fingers. The air grew colder with each step, the temperature dropping as if the house itself was trying to warn them away.

The door was still there, hidden beneath a thin layer of cracked plaster, its outline faint but undeniable. Edward reached out, his fingers brushing against the cold wall, the texture rough beneath his skin. The house seemed to hold its breath, the silence pressing tight against his ears.

Joseph handed him the crowbar without a word.

The first strike echoed through the attic like a gunshot, the sound sharp and jarring in the stillness. The plaster crumbled easily, falling away in brittle chunks, revealing the rotting wood beneath—an old door, small and narrow, the wood dark with age, the edges warped from years of being hidden.

There was no handle. Just a faint indentation where one might have been, as if it had been removed deliberately.

Edward hesitated, his heart pounding, then slid the crowbar into the gap and pried the door open.

It groaned softly, the sound low and guttural, as if the house itself was protesting.

Behind the door was darkness. Not the absence of light, but something heavier—a thick, suffocating void that seemed to swallow the weak glow from their lanterns.

Edward stepped forward, his breath shallow, the air colder than it had any right to be. The space beyond the door was small, more of a crawlspace than a room, the walls lined with old wooden beams, their surfaces etched with faint, crude carvings —symbols he didn't recognize, sharp and jagged, like they'd been scratched into the wood in a hurry.

In the center of the space sat a small wooden box.

It was simple, unremarkable, but the sight of it made Edward's chest tighten, his skin prickling with a cold that had nothing to do with the temperature.

Joseph stepped beside him, his voice low. "Well, are you going to open it?"

Edward didn't answer. He just reached out, his fingers trembling slightly as he lifted the lid.

Inside, wrapped in brittle, yellowed cloth, was a small bundle of papers—letters, old and fragile, their edges browned with age.

And beneath them—something else.

A small, rusted key.

Edward stared at it, his heart pounding in his chest, the faint whispers from the house growing louder in the silence.

He didn't sleep that night.

None of them did.

CHAPTER TWENTY

The night had been long, its hours stretched thin like fragile fabric pulled taut over something sharp. By morning, the weak light creeping through the stained and cracked windows felt like an intrusion, unwelcome and indifferent to the restless hearts it illuminated. The house itself seemed resentful of the dawn, its timbers groaning softly as if reluctant to let go of whatever it had held during the dark hours.

Edward sat at the kitchen table, his fingers resting on the small, rusted key they'd found in the attic. It was unremarkable in appearance—simple, tarnished with age, its once-smooth surface now pitted and scarred. But there was a weight to it that defied its size, as if it carried more than just the promise of unlocking something physical. It felt like it belonged to the house, or worse, like the house belonged to it.

The letters were spread out before him, fragile sheets of parchment stained with time, the ink faded but still legible. He hadn't read them yet. There was a hesitation in his chest, a fear that the words would confirm something he wasn't ready to face. The silence in the kitchen was thick, broken only by the faint, persistent ticking of the old clock on the wall, though neither he nor Joseph could remember winding it.

Joseph entered with his usual restless energy, though it was frayed at the edges now, his movements sharp in a way that suggested exhaustion more than impatience. His eyes landed on the key immediately, a flicker of something—curiosity or dread—passing through his expression before he masked it with the usual indifference.

"That little thing's caused quite a stir," he muttered, pouring himself a cup of coffee that had gone cold hours ago.

Edward didn't respond, his fingers tracing the edges of the key, feeling the faint grooves worn into the metal.

Joseph pulled out a chair, the legs scraping loudly against the uneven floorboards, and sat across from him. "So, what's the plan? We going to sit here staring at it all day, or are we going to find out what it opens?"

Edward's jaw tightened. "I'm not sure I want to know."

Joseph snorted, leaning back in his chair. "Since when has 'not wanting to know' stopped us from doing anything?"

The key sat between them like a fragile truce, the space around it filled with more tension than either of them cared to acknowledge.

Meg found them like that, the air between her brothers thick with unspoken words and the faint undercurrent of fear they wouldn't admit out loud. She didn't say anything at first, just moved to the table and picked up one of the letters, her fingers careful against the brittle paper.

The handwriting was sharp and precise, the ink faded but still strong enough to carry the weight of its message. The letter was addressed to Josiah Darlington, the name etched with a kind of reverence—or perhaps warning—that made her skin crawl. She read aloud, her voice soft but steady, filling the silence with words meant to be forgotten:

"The debt is paid in blood, as it was promised. The land remembers, even when we do not."

She lowered the letter slowly, her breath shallow, the words lingering in the room like ash after a fire.

Joseph laughed, but it was hollow, brittle around the edges. "Well, that's comforting."

Edward stood abruptly, the chair scraping harshly against the floor. "There's something in this house," he said, his voice low but firm, as if saying it aloud gave it more shape, more substance. "Something tied to this key. To these letters. And to us."

Meg met his gaze, her eyes sharp. "Then we find it."

They started with the attic, retracing their steps, the air colder than it had been the night before. The faint outline of the hidden door still marked the wall, the space behind it empty now, but somehow it felt even more oppressive without the box sitting there. The darkness seemed to press inward, thick and heavy, as if the house resented the intrusion.

The key felt cold in Edward's hand, its weight growing heavier with each step as they searched for something—anything—it might unlock. They moved through the house in silence, the old floorboards groaning under their feet, the walls seeming to watch them with the same disinterest as the faded portraits lining the halls.

It wasn't until they reached the basement door—a narrow, warped thing half-hidden behind an old cabinet—that

Edward felt it. A faint pull, like a thread tugging at the edge of his mind, urging him forward.

The door had been locked for as long as any of them could remember, the key lost—or so they'd thought.

Edward slid the key into the lock.

It fit perfectly.

The click of the mechanism releasing was louder than it should have been, echoing down the narrow hall like a gunshot in the quiet.

Joseph stepped back slightly, his posture tense. "After you," he muttered, trying to mask the fear in his voice with a smirk that didn't quite reach his eyes.

Edward opened the door.

The darkness beyond was absolute, swallowing the weak light from the hallway, thick and heavy like it had been waiting. The air was colder here, sharp and damp, carrying the faint scent of earth and something else—something metallic, like rust or blood.

Meg lit a lantern, its flickering glow casting long, thin shadows that danced along the crumbling stone walls as they descended the narrow stairs. The space below was small, the ceiling low, forcing them to stoop as they moved deeper. The floor was dirt, uneven and damp, with patches of frost lingering despite the walls sheltering it from the winter air.

And in the center of the room was a trunk.

Old, wooden, the metal hinges rusted, the surface scarred with faint markings—symbols similar to those carved into the beams in the attic.

Edward approached slowly, his heart pounding, the key still warm in his hand. He knelt, fitting the key into the lock.

It turned easily.

The trunk creaked open, the sound sharp in the oppressive silence.

Inside, beneath layers of rotting fabric, were bones.

Small.

Fragile.

Human.

And tucked between them—another letter.

Edward didn't read it. Not yet.

Because the house had gone silent.

And something was standing in the doorway.

CHAPTER
TWENTY-ONE

The basement air was oppressive, thick with dampness and the lingering scent of decaying wood and rusted metal that clung to every breath they took. Edward crouched beside the ancient trunk, its hinges corroded and its wood scarred by time. His fingers hesitated above the brittle letter, the faded ink a ghostly whisper against the yellowed parchment. Joseph stood rigidly behind him, arms crossed, his usual bravado flickering like a candle in the darkness. His voice, low and raw, broke the silence. "What debt? What the hell does that mean?"

Edward's voice was barely above a whisper. "I don't know."

Meg knelt beside them, her eyes locked on the fragile bones arranged with unsettling care in the trunk. Her voice trembled. "It's not just who did this, but why." She reached out, fingers hovering above the delicate remains as if the bones themselves could speak. The basement walls felt closer now, the shadows thicker, more alive. Edward swallowed hard. "We shouldn't be here," he muttered. Yet none of them moved.

When they finally ascended the narrow stairs, each step creaked beneath their weight, a sound that felt less like settling wood and more like a warning. The parlor felt no safer. The letter, now spread across the table, seemed to pulse with a malevolent presence. Edward collapsed into a worn armchair, exhaustion carving deep lines into his face. Joseph poured himself a drink with shaking hands, the clink of glass betraying his fear. Meg's voice echoed softly. "The land takes what it's owed." Edward's eyes narrowed. "Debt for what?" She met his gaze, her own sharp despite the fear that shimmered within. "For everything buried here. For everything done to keep this land."

That night, sleep was a distant hope. Edward's restless pacing filled the narrow hallway, the rusted key cold and unyielding in his pocket. Meg's room, illuminated by the faint glow of moonlight, was a sea of sketches. She looked up as Edward entered. "They're maps," she whispered. He knelt beside her, tracing the jagged lines. "Maps of what?" Her answer was barely audible. "The land remembers, Edward." His murmur echoed hers. "Maybe the house isn't the only thing hiding secrets." Her voice, fragile but firm, responded, "Maybe the land itself is keeping count."

CHAPTER
TWENTY-TWO

The basement air pressed down on them like a tangible weight, thick with the mingling scents of damp earth, decaying wood, and something metallic that lingered like the memory of blood. Edward's fingers trembled around the brittle letter, each faded word a sharp incision into the fabric of their fragile understanding. The land takes what is owed. The debt is never forgiven. Only forgotten. The letters felt like scars on the page, ancient wounds that never healed. Joseph stood stiffly beside him, arms crossed in a futile attempt to shield himself from the realization creeping into the edges of his bravado. His voice broke the silence, rough and strained, as though forcing the words out might keep the fear at bay. "What debt? What the hell does that mean?" His voice bounced off the crumbling walls and dissolved into the cold darkness.

Meg's wide, glassy eyes remained fixed on the fragile bones nestled in the rotting trunk, her voice a thin thread of sound. "It's not just about who did this," she whispered.

"It's about why." Edward could feel the weight of her words settle into his chest, heavy and undeniable. The basement seemed to breathe around them, each shadow shifting, each corner darkening, as if the house itself was listening. Edward swallowed hard, the metallic tang of fear coating his throat. "We shouldn't be down here," he muttered, but none of them moved.

When they finally climbed the narrow stairs, the house greeted them with a groan, the floorboards creaking as if under the strain of their new knowledge. In the parlor, the letter lay spread across the table, an ominous presence that seemed to pulse with its own dark energy. Edward sank into a worn armchair, exhaustion etching new lines into his face. Joseph poured a drink, the clink of glass on bottle betraying the slight tremor in his hand. "The land takes what it's owed," Meg repeated, her voice distant, hollow. Edward looked at her sharply. "Debt for what?" The fire crackled softly, casting shifting shadows that danced across the faded wallpaper. Meg's eyes, sharp despite her fear, locked onto his. "For everything buried here. For everything done to keep this land."

Sleep remained elusive. Edward paced the narrow hallway, the small rusted key a cold weight in his pocket. Its presence was an unspoken demand. His thoughts churned, circling around the letter, the bones, and the unseen force binding them to Darlington House. Drawn by an inexplicable urge, he found Meg awake in her room, surrounded by sketches that covered the floor like scattered pieces of a puzzle. She didn't look up. "They're maps," she whispered. Edward knelt beside her, tracing the lines with a trembling finger. "Maps of what?" She exhaled softly. "The land remembers, Edward." His voice was a murmur, more to himself than to her. "Maybe the house isn't the only thing hiding secrets." Meg's voice, barely audible, replied, "Maybe the land itself is keeping count."

CHAPTER TWENTY-THREE

The days at Darlington House began to merge into one unbroken stretch of unease, time measured not by clocks or sunsets but by the growing weight pressing down from the very walls and floors. The house groaned louder, not with age, but with the burden of memory too long repressed. Edward stood at the parlor window, the frost painting delicate veins across the glass, mirroring the cracks within him. His reflection stared back, gaunt and haunted, a man unraveling thread by thread. The rusted key in his pocket felt heavier than any metal should, as though it carried the weight of every unspoken truth buried within these walls.

Outside, the north field stretched out like a scar under the overcast sky, the soil dark and stubborn, holding secrets no one dared speak aloud. Joseph, slumped in an armchair, swirled the remnants of whiskey in his glass, the embers in the hearth casting flickering shadows that danced like ghosts. His usual sarcasm had dulled into a quiet bitterness, an edge sharpened by sleepless nights and unanswered questions. Meg sat cross-legged near the fire, her sketchbook open but untouched, filled with maps and symbols drawn from somewhere deeper than memory, her fingers absently tracing lines she didn't remember drawing.

The silence was more than absence—it was presence, heavy and palpable, as if the house itself was holding its breath. Edward's voice sliced through it, low and certain. "We need to go back."

Joseph's eyes flicked up, his smirk hollow. "Back to what? Another box of bones? More letters telling us we're cursed?"

Edward's jaw clenched. "Back to find answers."

Meg's whisper barely reached them. "The land remembers."

The basement air wrapped around them like a shroud, damp and cold, each step down the creaking stairs an admission of their own fear. Edward's lantern cast thin beams across the dirt floor, illuminating the marks Meg had found—spirals, symbols, carvings in the earth that felt older than the house itself. Kneeling, she brushed away the soil, revealing a small, dark wooden box, etched with the same crude symbols from her sketches. Edward's hand trembled as he fit the key into the lock, the box resisting as if unwilling to give up its secrets.

Inside were letters brittle with age, and an iron pendant shaped like an eye, its surface rough with time. Meg's breath hitched. "I've drawn this," she whispered. Page after page of her sketches showed the same symbol, woven into the house's outline, hidden in the corners of her maps.

In the parlor, Edward read aloud from the letters, the

words cutting through the room's fragile calm. "The land takes what is owed. The debt is never forgiven." Joseph's voice was sharp with frustration. "Debt for what?" Meg's fingers tightened around the pendant. "For everything buried here. For everything done to keep this land."

Edward's stare was distant, lost in the fire's glow. "Whatever we've uncovered, it's not finished with us."

CHAPTER TWENTY-FOUR

Morning seeped through Darlington House like a hesitant intruder, its weak, gray light barely penetrating the thick shroud of shadows that clung to the walls. The frost feathering across the windows resembled delicate fractures, beautiful yet unyielding, much like the weight of secrets pressing down upon those trapped within the house's decaying embrace. Every creak of the wooden floors felt deliberate, every sigh of the walls an unspoken confession.

Edward leaned against the cold kitchen sink, his fingers tight around a mug of coffee that had long since gone cold. His reflection in the frost-blurred window stared back, gaunt and haunted, the eyes of a man carrying too much. Beyond the glass, the north field stretched wide and barren, its dark soil holding stories no one dared speak aloud. The memory of the basement lingered—fragile bones, forgotten letters, and that iron pendant with its single, unblinking eye. Even now, it rested on the worn table behind him, its gaze a silent demand.

Joseph entered with the shuffle of someone who hadn't truly slept in weeks, his hand rough against the stubble on his jaw, the faint scent of whiskey clinging to him like a second skin. "We going to talk about it?" he muttered, his voice carrying the brittle edge of a man trying too hard to sound indifferent. "Or are we just gonna keep pretending there isn't a box of bones in the basement?"

Edward turned, his eyes steady but distant. "We need to know why it's there. Why this land won't let us go."

Joseph let out a hollow laugh, slumping into a chair. "Why? So we can sleep better? Spoiler alert: we won't."

Meg's voice cut through the tension like a whisper through still air. She stood in the doorway, her sketchbook clutched tightly in her hands, pages smudged with charcoal fingerprints. "Because it's not just about us. It's about the land. And whatever it wants... it's watching." She laid the sketchbook on the table, flipping through pages filled with the same ominous eye drawn over and over.

The day unraveled in uneasy fragments. Edward split firewood with a methodical, almost desperate precision, each swing of the axe echoing like a heartbeat. Joseph mended the sagging fence, driving nails harder than necessary, as if trying to hammer out his frustration. Meg scrubbed the wooden floors until her hands ached, but no amount of cleaning could erase the stains only they could see.

That evening, the fire crackled softly as they gathered in the parlor, the silence between them thick with unspoken fears. Edward sat on the edge of his chair, the iron pendant in his hand, its rough surface biting into his palm. "We're tethered," he whispered, his voice low but certain. "To this house. To the land.

To what's buried here."

Joseph drained his glass, the bitterness in his tone cutting deeper than his words. "I never asked for any of this."

Edward's eyes hardened. "It doesn't matter. It's ours now. The debt was signed in blood long before we got here."

Meg, curled in the corner with her sketchbook, spoke softly but firmly. "We can't leave. Even if we tried... it wouldn't let us."

Sleep never came that night. Edward found himself outside at dawn, the frost biting his skin, his breath a thin mist in the cold air. The field stretched before him, silent and still.

And at the far edge, a figure stood. Unmoving. Watching.

Edward's heart pounded, but he didn't move. Neither did the figure.

Both bound by the weight of history and the unseen threads of a debt that refused to be forgotten.

CHAPTER
TWENTY-FIVE

Dawn settled over Darlington House like a hesitant promise, its fragile light barely cutting through the mist that clung to the land. Edward stood at the edge of the north field, his breath a shallow mist curling in the cold air. The figure he had seen before sunrise was gone, but its presence lingered in the silence, an unsettling echo that gnawed at him. The earth beneath him felt unsettlingly soft, as if something beneath the surface stirred, waiting to rise.

Meg's soft voice broke the silence from the porch. "Did you see it again?" She didn't need an answer. Her tired eyes, shadowed with too many sleepless nights, met his across the brittle yard. They both knew.

Inside, the weight of unseen eyes pressed against the walls. Edward stood in the kitchen with Joseph and Meg, his voice steady despite the unease in his chest. "We need to leave. Just for a little while." Joseph's sharp laugh cut through the tension. "And go where? This town doesn't forget who we are." Meg, fingers smudged with charcoal from her sketches, whispered, "It's not about the house anymore. It's the land."

The road to Dover's Hollow was rough, each jolt of Joseph's old truck feeling like a struggle against invisible hands holding them back. The town, unchanged yet foreign, greeted them with lingering stares and half-remembered whispers. The diner, a small refuge of warmth, felt fragile against the cold weight they carried. Lena, the waitress, offered a knowing glance, her silence saying more than words could.

The door's bell jingled, and a man stepped in, his presence cutting through the hum of morning chatter. Silas Boone, tall and weathered, locked eyes with Edward. "Darlington House," he said softly, as if the name itself carried a curse. Joseph's sarcastic retort hung in the air, but Silas's quiet reply froze them all. "The land remembers. And it doesn't forgive."

Their conversation stretched long, Silas revealing pieces of a history darker than they had imagined—debt paid in blood, promises etched into the soil, and the Darlington name bound to it all. Meg's fingers traced the worn edges of her sketchbook, her voice barely above a whisper. "We need to know everything." Silas's eyes, gray like storm clouds, held them captive. "You might not want to."

Edward's voice, steady yet strained, replied, "We don't have a choice." The shadows outside the diner's windows thickened, as if the land itself listened, waiting.

CHAPTER
TWENTY-SIX

T he days following their encounter with Silas Boone stretched long and uneasy, each hour weighed down by the memory of his parting words: "The land remembers. And it doesn't forgive." Edward found himself pacing the narrow halls of Darlington House more than ever, the weight of unseen eyes pressing against him, the walls groaning with secrets too old to name. Even the light that filtered through the windows felt dimmer, as though reluctant to touch what lay within.

It was a week later when the invitation arrived, a thick envelope left at the front door, its edges gilded and name unfamiliar. Meg found it, her fingers tracing the elegant script. She brought it to Edward and Joseph in the kitchen, where the scent of stale coffee lingered in the air. Joseph raised an eyebrow as Edward read aloud, "You are cordially invited to the annual Winter's Crest Ball at Willowmere Estate. Formal attire required." Beneath, a single name: Annabelle Langston.

Joseph scoffed. "A ball? Really? Nothing like pretending we're not cursed while drinking punch with people who whisper about us behind our backs."

Edward's lips twitched, but his eyes remained thoughtful. "Willowmere is older than Darlington. The Langstons have been here longer than we have. Maybe... maybe they know something."

Meg, still clutching the envelope, whispered, "Or maybe it's exactly what we need—a chance to breathe."

The night of the ball arrived with a sharp wind that sliced through the barren fields. Willowmere Estate stood tall and untouched by time, its white columns gleaming against the night sky. Inside, chandeliers dripped with crystal, and the soft strains of a string quartet filled the air. Edward adjusted his suit—too crisp, too unfamiliar—while Joseph's tie hung loose and his sleeves were rolled just enough to show his disdain for formalities. Meg, in a dark green gown that made her eyes sharper than ever, looked around with cautious curiosity.

Edward's gaze locked on a figure near the grand staircase. Clara Langston. Her sapphire gown clung to her as if it were part of her, her dark eyes catching the light like shards of glass. Their eyes met, and for a moment, Edward felt the noise around them fade.

"You're Edward Darlington," she said when they finally stood face to face.

"And you're Clara Langston."

"I've heard stories," she murmured, her smile faint.

"Everyone has."

"I prefer truths," she whispered back. "And I think you

carry more than your share."

The night stretched long, whispers of the past mingling with music, until Edward finally asked, "Why invite us?"

Clara's gaze hardened. "Because the land doesn't forgive. But sometimes… it offers a chance to understand."

As the clock neared midnight, Edward knew one thing for certain: the land remembered, and it wasn't done with them yet.

CHAPTER TWENTY-SEVEN

The grand ballroom of Willowmere Estate was a cathedral of elegance, where light cascaded from glittering chandeliers and bathed the polished marble floors in a soft glow. Conversations ebbed and flowed like a tide, punctuated by the gentle clinking of crystal glasses and the delicate strains of a string quartet weaving through the air. The scent of beeswax candles mingled with expensive perfume, the faintest breath of winter slipping through the tall windows to remind guests that, beyond this opulence, the cold still waited.

Edward Darlington felt the weight of the room pressing against him, though his focus was anchored to one point alone —Clara Langston. She moved through the crowd with a grace that felt both natural and deliberate, her sapphire gown a stark contrast to the warm golds and creams of the room. There was a sharpness to her beauty, a precision in her every glance and smile that suggested she saw more than most and cared less than she should. Edward's thoughts tangled as he watched her, drawn not just by attraction but by something deeper, something unsettlingly familiar.

"You're going to wear a hole in the floor with that pacing," Joseph muttered from behind him, nursing a glass of bourbon, his tie already loosened despite the formal setting.

Edward glanced at him, lips curving in a faint smirk. "And you're going to wear out your liver with that drinking."

Joseph grinned, raising his glass in mock salute. "We all cope differently, brother."

Meg, perched at the edge of the dance floor, leaned in with a teasing glint in her eye. "You could always just talk to her, you know. Instead of staring like a lovesick ghost."

Edward chuckled softly, shaking his head. "It's not that simple."

"Nothing ever is with us," Meg replied, her voice holding a trace of melancholy.

But before Edward could respond, Clara's laughter—a soft, musical sound that seemed to thread through the noise—reached him, and something inside him shifted. Without another word, he crossed the room.

When he reached her, Clara's gaze slid to his, unflinching and amused. "Mr. Darlington," she greeted, her voice smooth as silk. "I was beginning to think you preferred brooding from afar."

Edward's lips twitched. "I don't brood."

She arched a brow. "No? Then what would you call that intense look you've been giving me?"

"Curiosity," he answered softly.

"And what are you curious about?" she asked, her eyes glinting.

Edward's hesitation lasted only a moment. "Why a woman like you would be interested in a man like me."

Clara leaned in, her voice a whisper against his ear. "Maybe I like men with shadows."

The air thickened between them, tension simmering beneath their polished exteriors. Edward extended his hand. "Dance with me."

Her smile deepened. "I thought you'd never ask."

They moved across the floor with fluidity, their steps perfectly synchronized, but it was the words unspoken that danced between them. Clara's touch was light yet grounding, and Edward found himself drawn into her orbit completely. As they swayed, she murmured, "Why are you really here, Edward?"

"To breathe," he admitted. "To remember what it feels like to be more than haunted."

Clara's fingers tightened on his. "Careful. Men who seek peace often find something else."

Edward's gaze locked onto hers. "I'm not looking for peace. I'm looking for truth."

Later, on the terrace, the cold night air bit at their skin, but neither moved away from it. "Do you believe in ghosts, Clara?" Edward asked softly.

"I believe in echoes," she replied. "And the things we can't bury."

"What do you carry?" he asked.

"Regret," she whispered.

Edward brushed a curl from her face, his touch lingering. But the sound of footsteps broke the moment. Silas Boone stood in the shadows, his expression grave. "We need to talk."

Edward's jaw tightened, but when he glanced at Clara, she wasn't surprised.

She was expecting it.

CHAPTER TWENTY-EIGHT

The night air on the terrace of Willowmere Estate clung to the bones with an icy precision, but Edward Darlington felt none of it, his mind still trapped in the lingering warmth of Clara Langston's touch, her presence more haunting than any ghost he had faced. Yet the moment shattered like brittle glass as Silas Boone's rough voice sliced through the fragile quiet. Edward turned, his expression sharp, his body taut with unspoken tension. Silas stood like a shadow barely tethered to the world, his weathered coat dusted with road grit, and boots that spoke of restless miles traveled with no destination.

Edward's gaze flicked to Clara, noting the mask that slipped so easily over her features—a mask of practiced calm that couldn't quite hide the flicker of recognition in her eyes. It was a flicker that twisted in Edward's chest like a thorn.

"You know him," Edward said, more statement than question.

Clara's voice was steady, but her eyes betrayed her. "I do."

Silas's mouth curled into a half-smile, void of warmth. "We've all got ghosts, Darlington. Some are just better at hiding them."

The weight of unspoken truths thickened the air, pressing against Edward's chest. He forced himself to stay still, his questions coiling tightly within him, waiting to strike. Clara, breaking the silence, whispered, "Not here."

In a small, dimly lit room lined with old books, the three faced each other, the scent of leather bindings and dust mingling with the tension crackling between them. Clara paced, her fingers brushing over worn spines as if searching for forgotten words. Edward leaned against the door, arms crossed, watching her. Silas, by the window, was a silhouette against the moonlit night, unreadable.

Clara spoke first, her voice quiet but cutting through the silence. "Annabelle Langston isn't my sister. She's my aunt. My mother died when I was young. Annabelle raised me because it was expected. Appearances are everything."

Edward processed her words but found no solace in them. "And Silas?" he asked.

Clara's glance at Silas was fleeting but filled with something Edward couldn't ignore—guilt. "We knew each other long before Willowmere."

Silas chuckled darkly. "Unfinished business."

Jealousy flared within Edward, but he tamped it down. There were deeper shadows to unravel.

"The Langstons," Clara continued, "aren't just old money —they're old blood. Like your family. But they've hidden their sins better."

Edward's voice was low, controlled. "Why tell me this now?"

Her answer was soft but unwavering. "Because whatever haunts Darlington House doesn't begin or end there."

Outside Willowmere, beneath an indifferent sky strewn with stars, Edward whispered, "Why do I feel like I'm drowning around you?"

Clara's answer was a breath against the cold. "Because you forgot how to breathe."

Their kiss was not gentle but desperate, a collision of broken pieces trying to fit. When they parted, Clara whispered, "This doesn't fix anything."

Edward's touch lingered. "I don't want to fix it."

And maybe that was the truest thing he'd ever said.

CHAPTER
TWENTY-NINE

The dawn after the Willowmere ball seeped through the cracked windows of Darlington House, casting weak beams across dust-laden floorboards that groaned under the weight of memories too heavy to hold. Edward Darlington stood at the edge of the north field, the frost-covered earth beneath his boots crunching softly, a stark contrast to the swirling storm in his mind. The figure he had seen at sunrise was gone, leaving behind only the unsettling feeling that something—or someone—had watched him, marking him like the land itself did every Darlington who dared to remain tethered to it.

When Edward returned to the kitchen, Joseph sat hunched over the table, a cigarette dangling from his fingers, its smoke curling upward in lazy tendrils. His eyes, bloodshot and rimmed with sleeplessness, flicked toward Edward.

"She's trouble," Joseph muttered, not needing to name Clara Langston.

Edward's voice was low, steady. "She knows more than we do. About the land. About us."

Joseph's dry chuckle was devoid of humor. "That's what makes her trouble."

Later, Edward found himself drawn back to Willowmere, the weight of unanswered questions and Clara's lingering touch pulling him. The Langston estate, pristine and grand, stood in stark contrast to the decaying bones of Darlington House, a facade of elegance masking something darker. Clara met him in the library, her figure framed by the pale afternoon light filtering through tall windows. Her mask of poise cracked just enough for Edward to see the weariness beneath.

"You came back," she said softly.

"You owe me answers," Edward replied.

Clara's faint smile held no joy. "Be careful with answers, Edward. They come with a price."

They sat by the fire, its warmth doing little to dispel the chill between them. Clara's voice trembled with the weight of her confession. "My mother fled this place, hoping to escape the darkness. But the land doesn't forget. It took her. And my father... he disappeared when I was a child. No one ever found him."

Edward reached for her hand, their fingers intertwining, grounding him to something real amidst the unraveling chaos.

That night, Edward's dreams were restless, filled with cracked soil and voices whispering in forgotten tongues. The key in his palm felt colder, heavier. And when Silas Boone arrived at dawn, leading him to a half-buried marker etched with the Darlington name and the year 1863, Edward's breath caught.

It wasn't just Darlington House that held secrets. It was the land itself, soaked in blood and memory, unwilling to forgive.

CHAPTER THIRTY

The days after the grave's discovery passed with a relentless weight that pressed against the very walls of Darlington House, each moment stretched thin by questions that offered no answers. Edward found himself drawn to the cracked stone marker beneath the ancient oak, the name carved into its surface a haunting echo that refused to be ignored. Darlington. The letters, weathered but distinct, whispered of a history he didn't know, and the date—1863— gnawed at the edges of his sanity. There had been no record, no mention of another Edward Darlington from that time. Yet the grave was undeniable, its presence a testament to something buried far deeper than bone.

In the quiet, Edward paced the kitchen floor, the rhythmic tapping of his boots the only sound as Joseph leaned against the counter, a cigarette smoldering between his fingers. "You keep circling the same questions," Joseph muttered, exhaling smoke that curled into the dim light. "Maybe it's time to start getting some damn answers."

Edward's voice was tight. "From who? The dead?"

Joseph's dry chuckle held no humor. "If anyone could, it'd be you."

The invitation arrived like a blade, sharp and unexpected, its parchment crisp and pristine, untouched by time's decay. Annabelle Langston's familiar script beckoned them to Willowmere once more, this time for a garden luncheon that promised more than idle conversation. Edward's grip tightened on the invitation as Meg looked on, her eyes reflecting a concern she rarely voiced.

"We shouldn't go," she whispered.

"We don't have a choice," Edward replied.

The day of the gathering was deceptively beautiful, the clear sky and warm sun a cruel contrast to the cold weight settled in Edward's chest. Willowmere's grounds, manicured and perfect, were a world away from the withering decay of Darlington House. Annabelle greeted them with a smile too practiced, her eyes lingering on Edward like a predator studying prey. "Welcome," she purred. "I was beginning to think you'd forgotten your manners."

Edward's lips barely curved. "Some things are hard to forget."

Clara was there, her burgundy gown a striking contrast to the lush greenery, but her eyes held a distance that unsettled Edward. They found themselves beneath an ancient magnolia tree, the shade cool against their skin.

"Why did you come back?" Edward asked quietly.

Clara's voice was a fragile thread. "Because the past doesn't let go."

Before Edward could respond, Silas Boone's figure

appeared like a shadow slipping through the cracks of the world. "You need to see something," he said, his voice low and urgent.

The woods beyond Willowmere grew darker as they followed Silas to a small clearing. The earth was disturbed, and as Silas brushed away the soil, Edward's breath stilled. Bones. Fragile, ancient, marked by crude symbols. Clara's voice trembled. "What is this?"

Silas's eyes were cold. "It's where the Langstons buried their debts."

The ride home was silent, but Edward's mind churned. "This isn't just about us," he whispered. "It's the land." Clara's hand found his, her voice barely audible. "And the blood that keeps it alive."

CHAPTER
THIRTY-ONE

The night hung over Darlington House like a veil woven from whispers and forgotten promises, the darkness clinging to every corner, pressing into the spaces between breaths. Edward sat alone in the dimly lit parlor, the flickering glow of an oil lamp casting shifting shadows that seemed to reach for him. The cracked stone marker from the woods haunted him still, its weathered inscription—Darlington, 1863—an unanswered question that gnawed at the fragile seams of his sanity. There was no record, no explanation, and yet, the earth had given up its secret, unbidden and undeniable.

He turned the rusted key over in his hand, feeling its weight, heavier than metal had any right to be, as though it carried the burdens of every door it had ever opened. Clara's voice echoed in his mind: "It's about the land. And the blood that keeps it fed." The memory of her words clung to him like smoke, impossible to brush away.

Sleep was an elusive phantom that night, and when it

finally came, it brought no peace—only dreams that felt more like memories borrowed from another life.

In the dream, Edward was not himself but Thomas Darlington, an ancestor whose name was barely a whisper in the family's annals. The world around him was a tapestry of 1863—blood-orange sunsets over parched fields, the grand Darlington Plantation standing pristine against time's eventual decay. Thomas stood on the porch, his hands stained with more than soil, his gaze haunted by guilt too heavy to carry. Inside, laughter drifted from the parlor, light and melodic, but sharp-edged—Isolde Langston's laughter. She was fierce, beautiful, and forbidden. Their love was a thread pulled too taut, ready to snap. Edward felt Thomas's anguish, the weight of betrayal, and the inescapable pull of the land beneath his feet.

Edward jolted awake, breathless, the dream's tendrils still wrapped around him. The key on the side table was unnaturally warm to the touch.

When he recounted the dream to Clara and Silas the next morning, Clara's face paled. "Isolde Langston was my great-great-grandmother," she whispered.

Silas's gaze darkened. "And Thomas Darlington was yours," he said to Edward. "This isn't just about land. It's about blood. Your blood."

Determined to unravel the truth, they returned to the attic where Edward unearthed a hidden journal—Thomas Darlington's words written in faded ink: "The land hungers, and we have fed it. But the debt grows, like roots beneath the soil, unseen but unyielding."

Clara's voice trembled. "They didn't just bury bodies. They buried sins."

Silas's jaw clenched. "And the land remembers."

The journal revealed rituals, sacrifices, and a blood-bound contract between the Darlington and Langston families, echoing through generations.

"This isn't just a curse," Edward whispered. "It's a contract."

Clara's hand found his, cold and certain. "And it's still active."

CHAPTER THIRTY-TWO

The road to Dover's Hollow stretched endlessly, a winding scar through the dense woods that whispered secrets too ancient to name. Edward Darlington gripped the wheel tightly, his knuckles pale, the engine's low rumble the only sound in the heavy silence that filled the truck. Shadows from the towering oaks and pines twisted in the headlights, casting fleeting shapes that seemed almost human, flickering specters that made Clara Langston glance uneasily into the darkness beyond the glass. Silas Boone, sitting beside her with an unsettling calm, stared straight ahead, his weathered face carved from stone, betraying nothing.

The tension inside the truck was palpable, each of them carrying questions too heavy to voice. Silas's voice finally cut through the silence, low and steady. "Dover's Hollow isn't just another forgotten town," he muttered, the words weighted with something more than memory.

Edward's eyes flicked to him in the rearview mirror.

"Then what is it?"

Silas leaned forward slightly, his voice almost a whisper. "It's where the land whispers the loudest."

The words settled over them like fog, creeping into the corners of their thoughts. Clara wrapped her arms around herself, shivering despite the steady hum of the truck's heater. "Whispers what?" she asked softly.

"That's what we're going to find out," Edward replied, his voice firm, though the weight of uncertainty pressed on his chest.

As they entered the town, Dover's Hollow revealed itself like a memory best left undisturbed. Buildings leaned with age, their wooden facades weathered and cracked, windows empty and dark like vacant eyes. The streets were deserted, the silence unnerving. It felt as though time had not just forgotten this place but abandoned it entirely.

Edward parked near a small, dilapidated shop with a barely legible sign: Granger's Books and Relics. "This is it," Silas said, stepping out into the brittle night air. Clara hesitated, her breath visible in the cold, before following. Edward locked the truck with a sharp click, scanning their surroundings with wary eyes.

Inside, the shop was a labyrinth of shelves crammed with ancient books, peculiar artifacts, and objects that seemed to hum with unseen energy. The scent of dust, leather, and old paper clung to the air. A single oil lamp flickered on a wooden counter, illuminating the sharp features of an old man with piercing eyes that seemed to see through time.

"Elias Granger," Edward greeted softly.

The old man's gaze moved from Edward to Clara to Silas, his expression unreadable. "Darlington," he said quietly, then nodded to Clara. "Langston." His eyes settled on Silas. "And the wanderer."

Silas's lips twitched into a faint smirk. "We need answers."

Granger studied them for a moment before gesturing to a room in the back, its walls lined with faded maps and ancient ledgers. He pulled a worn leather-bound book from a shelf, its spine cracked with age, and placed it before them. "This," he said, "is the history of your land. Not the one in your family records—the real one."

Edward opened the book with reverence, the delicate pages revealing names, dates, and symbols that made his heart pound. Clara leaned in, her breath catching as she traced the names with her fingertips. "Thomas Darlington and Isolde Langston," she whispered.

Granger's voice was low, steady. "Their love defied their families, but it was their desperation during the war that sealed the land's fate. Blood magic. A pact with the land to ensure survival."

Edward's voice was tight. "A pact?"

"A contract," Granger corrected. "One that demands blood to keep the land fertile and their wealth secure. But magic like that doesn't fade. It festers."

Clara's eyes darkened with realization. "And now it wants payment."

Granger's gaze was somber. "It never stopped wanting payment."

The ride back to Darlington House was silent, each lost in their thoughts, the weight of what they had learned pressing down like the sky itself had grown heavier. Edward's mind raced with questions, with dread. Clara stared out the window, her reflection ghostly in the glass, while Silas sat in contemplative silence.

As the truck approached the house, its dark silhouette looming against the moonlit sky, Edward whispered, "We have to end this."

Clara's reply was a mere breath, but its weight was undeniable. "Or it will end us."

CHAPTER THIRTY-THREE

The journey back from Dover's Hollow was steeped in an unbearable silence, each passing mile pulling Edward Darlington, Clara Langston, and Silas Boone deeper into the web of ancient curses and whispered secrets that now bound them. Edward's knuckles were taut against the steering wheel, his mind a torrent of questions that clawed for answers. Beside him, Clara sat rigid, her eyes lost in the passing shadows of gnarled branches, her breath shallow as if afraid to disturb the fragile quiet. In the backseat, Silas reclined with an unsettling calm, but his sharp gaze flickered between Edward and Clara, calculating, waiting.

"Elias Granger's words won't leave me," Edward muttered, breaking the silence, his voice hoarse. "A contract sealed in blood, binding the land to our sins. How did it come to this?"

Clara turned to him, her voice barely a whisper but laced with anguish. "We inherited this curse, Edward. Born into a debt we never signed, but one we're bound to pay." She clenched her fists in her lap, nails digging into her palms as if pain could anchor her.

Silas chuckled softly, a bitter sound that made Edward glance at him through the rearview mirror. "That's the thing about the past," Silas said, his voice low and gravelly. "It doesn't care who's holding the burden, as long as someone bleeds for it."

The truck's headlights sliced through the darkness, illuminating the twisted limbs of the forest that loomed like ancient sentinels. Each turn of the road felt heavier, as if the land itself resisted their return, its roots entwining with the curse they carried. Darlington House emerged through the mist, its silhouette a monstrous shadow against the night sky, the weight of centuries pressing down on its weathered frame.

Inside, the house greeted them with an unsettling stillness. Shadows stretched unnaturally along the wooden floors, and the flickering glow from the lanterns cast shapes that seemed to dance just beyond sight. Edward lit the fireplace, the flames flickering wildly, as though the house itself breathed through the fire.

"We need to know more," Edward said, his voice firm but strained. "We need to understand what the land wants from us."

Clara's gaze met his, her eyes reflecting both fear and determination. "Annabelle kept records," she whispered. "Everything is at Willowmere."

Silas leaned back against the wall, his smirk sharp as a blade. "Secrets wrapped in lace and hidden behind gilded doors. Typical Langstons."

The next morning, under a bleak sky, they made their

way to Willowmere Estate. Its grand columns and immaculate grounds stood in cruel contrast to the decay of Darlington House, a façade of perfection concealing centuries of rot. Clara led them through the opulent halls with hurried steps, stopping before a tall, locked door.

"Annabelle's study," she whispered, producing a small brass key from beneath a rug. The door creaked open, revealing shelves heavy with leather-bound books and stacks of parchment yellowed with age. The scent of lavender and old paper filled the air as Clara sifted through the clutter, pulling out a journal embossed with the Langston crest.

"This is it," she breathed, opening the journal to reveal pages filled with delicate script, symbols, and Latin inscriptions. "The blood contract." Her voice trembled. "It wasn't just a promise. It was a ritual, and it demands a price."

Edward's jaw clenched. "A price we've yet to fully pay."

Silas's eyes darkened, a humorless smile tugging at his lips. "The only question left is... who's next?"

The house, the land, the blood that bound them all—it was alive, waiting, hungry. And now, it knew their names.

CHAPTER THIRTY-FOUR

The weight of the journal's revelations lingered long after Edward Darlington, Clara Langston, and Silas Boone had returned from Willowmere, a suffocating presence that wrapped itself around Darlington House like ivy choking the life from ancient brick. Edward stood alone in the dimly lit hallway, his fingers tracing the rough edges of the journal, the Langston crest etched into the leather like a scar. The house, usually steeped in its familiar unease, now felt restless—its whispers louder, its shadows darker. Every groan of the old floorboards under Edward's weight echoed louder than it should, as if unseen eyes followed his every move.

Clara found him there, her presence quiet yet palpable, the weight of shared secrets pressing down on her shoulders. "You've read it again," she whispered, her voice a fragile thread in the stillness. "The contract. It's all we have, but it's not enough." She stepped closer, her fingers brushing against Edward's, the warmth of her touch grounding him. Her dark eyes, usually so fierce, were clouded with doubt.

"We need more," Edward replied, his voice low but resolute. "The journal tells us what was done, but not how to undo it. The land demands blood, and it's not finished with us."

A sudden, sharp knock shattered the fragile calm, reverberating through the house like a gunshot. Edward and Clara exchanged a glance heavy with dread. Slowly, Edward approached the front door, his heart pounding in rhythm with each knock. When he opened it, there was no one—only a single withered rose, its petals as dark as dried blood, lying on the doorstep.

"It knows," Clara breathed, barely audible. "It knows we're close."

The hours that followed blurred into a restless haze. Edward, Clara, and Silas gathered in the parlor, the flickering lantern casting elongated shadows that seemed to reach for them. Edward traced the edges of the journal while Clara read aloud, her voice trembling. "The blood spilled shall bind the earth and the heirs, until the debt is paid in full," she whispered. "This isn't just about land, Edward. It's about us."

The room grew colder, a chill settling into their bones as the faint sound of chains dragging across the wooden floor echoed through the hallway. Edward's breath hitched as a dark figure coalesced from the shadows, its hollow eyes and twisted face a silent scream of torment. Silas, usually unshakable, whispered, "We're not alone anymore."

The apparition's voice, a harsh whisper like wind through dry leaves, filled the room. "The debt... must be paid."

Edward clenched his fists, defiant. "We'll find another

way."

A cold, cruel laugh echoed through the walls, and the lantern sputtered out, plunging them into darkness.

The haunting wasn't coming. It was here.

CHAPTER THIRTY-FIVE

The weight of the journal's revelations pressed upon Edward Darlington with a suffocating intensity, each detail of the Langston crest and blood-stained history digging into his mind like thorns. The familiar unease of Darlington House had mutated into something far more sinister, each shadow sharper, each whisper louder. Edward stood in the dim corridor, the journal's worn leather binding a painful reminder of the burden he carried. Beneath him, the floorboards groaned not from age, but from something unseen, something stirring just beneath the surface.

Clara Langston approached quietly, her dark eyes reflecting the flickering candlelight and the unspoken fears they shared. Her voice, though soft, carried the weight of their predicament. "We know what they did, Edward. But how do we stop what they've started?" Her hand brushed his, lingering as if grounding herself in his presence, the only warmth in a house growing colder by the hour.

Edward's voice was low but steady, a mixture of resolve and dread. "The land wants what it's owed, Clara. Blood for blood. The question is—whose blood will it take?"

A sudden knock, sharp and relentless, shattered the stillness. Edward's heart pounded as he approached the front door, every creak beneath his feet amplified. He opened it to find nothing but a single withered rose, its petals blackened as though scorched by unseen flames.

Clara's breath hitched. "It knows, Edward. It knows we're close."

The night stretched on, heavy with tension. Edward, Clara, and Silas Boone gathered in the parlor, the lantern's flame flickering wildly, casting grotesque shadows that seemed to shift of their own accord. Clara's voice trembled as she read from the journal, "The blood spilled shall bind the earth and the heirs, until the debt is paid in full." She looked up, her voice breaking. "It's not just about the land. It's us, Edward. Our blood. Our lives."

The temperature plummeted, and the faint scrape of chains echoed through the walls. Edward's pulse raced as a figure emerged from the darkness, a spectral woman whose eyes were hollow voids and whose face twisted in eternal anguish. Silas, for once without a smirk, muttered, "We're not alone anymore."

The ghost's voice, brittle and haunting, filled the room. "The debt... must be paid."

Edward, jaw clenched, whispered fiercely, "We'll find another way."

A cold laugh resonated through the walls, the lantern sputtering out, leaving them engulfed in a darkness that breathed.

The haunting wasn't approaching. It had begun.

CHAPTER THIRTY-SIX

The darkness that clung to Darlington House was no longer a passive presence; it had become a malevolent force, pressing against the walls, curling through the halls like smoke from an unseen fire. Edward Darlington felt its weight with every breath, each step heavier than the last as he paced the parlor floor. The revelations from the journal—names soaked in blood, secrets tangled with roots as old as the land itself—echoed in his mind, unrelenting.

Clara Langston's silhouette, framed by the cold glow of the moon through the window, seemed fragile yet unyielding. She whispered, her voice almost lost to the silence, "I can hear them, Edward. Chains. Dragging through the floors beneath us."

He nodded, his voice grim. "They're not whispers anymore. They're warnings."

A sudden chill washed over them as the flickering light of the lantern trembled violently. Silas Boone appeared at the doorway, his usual nonchalance replaced by something sharper, more wary. "We've woken something we shouldn't have."

Before anyone could respond, an unseen force rattled the

walls, and a spectral figure materialized—a woman bound in rusted chains, her face obscured by a veil soaked in shadows. Her hollow eyes stared into their souls. "Blood for blood," she hissed, her voice slicing through the air like shards of broken glass.

Edward's jaw tightened. "What do you want from us?"

CHAPTER THIRTY-SEVEN

A suffocating stillness gripped Darlington House, heavier than the darkest midnight, pressing down on every creaking beam and ancient wall. Edward Darlington stood rigid at the top of the grand staircase, his knuckles white around the flickering lantern, its light casting trembling shadows that danced along the walls like restless phantoms. His gaze swept the dim hallway below, each shadow promising something unseen.

Clara Langston appeared at his side, her shawl drawn tightly around her as if to shield herself from the cold that wasn't entirely of this world. Her breath fogged the air, eyes wide with a mix of fear and resolve. "It's watching," she whispered, her voice barely audible, but Edward heard the truth in it.

He nodded, his voice a hushed murmur. "Not it. Them."

The staircase groaned under their hesitant steps, each creak a jarring sound in the unnerving silence. Silas Boone waited in the parlor, his usually smug expression replaced with grim determination. The fireplace was cold, its ashes undisturbed, yet the room's chill felt unnatural, as though something unseen drained every ounce of warmth.

"They're close," Silas muttered, scanning the dark corners of the room.

Edward set the lantern down on a worn table, its glow flickering wildly, casting elongated shadows that twisted unnaturally. Clara shivered, not from the cold, but from the weight of unseen eyes.

Then it came—the whisper. Faint at first, a breath on the back of the neck, then growing louder, swirling through the room like an invisible tide.

"Trapped... forgotten... bound by blood..."

Clara's hand tightened on Edward's arm, her voice cracking as she asked, "Who are you?"

The whisper became a mournful wail, chilling them to their core. Edward's breath caught as flickering faces appeared on the walls—gaunt, hollow-eyed, their expressions twisted in eternal sorrow.

"Those who came before... those who paid the price..."

Silas clenched his fists, his voice a harsh whisper. "The cursed ones. The souls bound here."

Edward swallowed hard. "The sacrificed."

The walls trembled as an unseen force swept through the room, extinguishing the lantern's feeble light. Darkness engulfed them, and Clara's gasp echoed through the void as Edward grasped her hand tightly.

A cold breath whispered against Edward's ear, its

bitterness unmistakable. "You will join us... soon."

Shadows pressed in closer, silent watchers with unseen eyes, their presence an unbearable weight. Then, a ghostly voice broke the silence: "We were bound... forgotten... buried beneath these branches."

Visions crashed into their minds—of chained souls brought from distant shores, their cries echoing through time, blood mingling with the cursed soil. Clara's eyes brimmed with tears as she whispered, "Our families did this... and we're left to pay."

The apparition's final words lingered as it dissolved into the shadows. "The land remembers. The blood demands its due."

Silas, his voice steady but grim, said, "We need every truth, every sin exposed. Or this place will devour us."

Edward, determination hardening his features, replied, "Then we start digging. And pray we survive what we unearth."

CHAPTER THIRTY-EIGHT

The weight of unseen eyes pressed heavily upon Darlington House, its ancient walls breathing with the memories of those who had come before—and those who had never left. Edward Darlington stood by the window, the faint glow of a flickering candle illuminating the sharp lines of his face, etched with exhaustion and determination. Outside, the land lay cloaked in mist, its once familiar expanse now foreign, as though time had unraveled, allowing the past to seep into the present.

Clara Langston, standing in the doorway, spoke softly, her voice fragile yet resolute. "It's the past," she whispered. "It's pulling us in."

Edward turned, meeting her gaze, his voice a low murmur. "No. It's dragging us under."

They moved through the house, each floorboard's groan a reluctant confession of the horrors it had witnessed. In the library, ancient tomes and forgotten artifacts stood as silent sentinels. Clara traced a finger over a faded map, whispering, "This land was never just land. It was a promise. A sacrifice."

A cold gust extinguished the candle, plunging them into darkness. Chains rattled faintly in the distance, and a voice—ancient, guttural—echoed through the room, "Blood for blood... debt unpaid..."

Visions struck them: dark ships on misty shores, anguished faces bound by iron, echoes of greed and stolen lives. Edward gasped, "They were never at rest."

Silas Boone entered, his tone grim. "We need their names. We need to remember them. Or they'll never leave."

Clara, her voice breaking, whispered, "And neither will we."

In the flickering light, Darlington House held its breath, waiting.

CHAPTER THIRTY-NINE

The weight of unseen eyes pressed heavily upon Darlington House, its ancient walls breathing with the memories of those who had come before—and those who had never left. Edward Darlington stood by the window, the faint glow of a flickering candle illuminating the sharp lines of his face, etched with exhaustion and determination. Outside, the land lay cloaked in mist, its once familiar expanse now foreign, as though time had unraveled, allowing the past to seep into the present.

Clara Langston, standing in the doorway, spoke softly, her voice fragile yet resolute. "It's the past," she whispered. "It's pulling us in."

Edward turned, meeting her gaze, his voice a low murmur. "No. It's dragging us under."

They moved through the house, each floorboard's groan a reluctant confession of the horrors it had witnessed. In the library, ancient tomes and forgotten artifacts stood as silent sentinels. Clara traced a finger over a faded map, whispering, "This land was never just land. It was a promise. A sacrifice."

A cold gust extinguished the candle, plunging them into darkness. Chains rattled faintly in the distance, and a voice— ancient, guttural—echoed through the room, "Blood for blood… debt unpaid…"

Visions struck them: dark ships on misty shores, anguished faces bound by iron, echoes of greed and stolen lives. Edward gasped, "They were never at rest."

Silas Boone entered, his tone grim. "We need their names. We need to remember them. Or they'll never leave."

Clara, her voice breaking, whispered, "And neither will we."

In the flickering light, Darlington House held its breath, waiting.

The weight of the journal's revelations clung to Edward long after they had left Willowmere, the Langston crest still burned into his mind. The land's hunger wasn't just an ancient tale—it was alive, breathing through the roots that twisted beneath the surface, waiting to claim what it was owed. Shadows stretched longer, whispers grew louder, and every creak of the floorboards seemed deliberate, as though the house itself strained under the weight of the past.

Clara stood by the window, her fingers trembling as she traced the frost-covered glass. "Edward," she whispered, her voice a fragile thread, "what if we can't stop it?"

His eyes darkened with resolve. "We have to."

Silas leaned against the doorway, arms crossed. "The past doesn't forgive easily," he muttered. "And neither do the dead."

The map Clara clutched marked an unvisited corner of the land—a forgotten place near the riverbend. "There's something there," she said softly. "Something they tried to hide."

Their journey through the woods was fraught with unseen eyes watching, the air thick with dread. When they reached the riverbend, an ancient altar stood before them, its stones stained dark with something far older than memory.

Suddenly, spectral figures emerged from the shadows, their faces contorted in anguish, bound by chains unseen yet palpable. "You cannot undo what has been done," they whispered. "Blood must pay for blood."

Edward's voice cut through the darkness. "We're here to end this."

Clara's hands trembled. "Then we'll give what it wants."

Silas's smirk vanished, replaced by a cold realization. "Not all of us will leave this place."

The altar pulsed with ancient energy, and Edward knew their time was running out.

The past demanded its due. And someone would have to pay.

CHAPTER FORTY

Darlington House stood as a silent sentinel against the storm-laden sky, its weathered timbers groaning beneath the weight of centuries. The air inside was thick with whispers and memories, each shadow holding its breath in anticipation. Edward Darlington sat in the library, the flicker of a lone candle casting wavering light across the open journal on the table before him. The words etched into the brittle pages seemed to pulse with an unsettling life of their own, recounting pacts sealed in blood, curses whispered through generations, and the unrelenting hunger of the land that bound them all.

Clara Langston paced near the window, her eyes distant and troubled. She pressed her hand to the glass, watching the mist curl around the skeletal trees outside. Her voice, when it came, was barely above a whisper. "I keep thinking about them… the ones who came before. Their pain is tethered to this place, to us."

Edward's gaze remained fixed on the journal. "We carry their weight now."

A sudden knock echoed through the house, sharp and insistent. Edward, Clara, and Silas Boone exchanged tense glances. Edward opened the door to find no one—only a yellowed envelope resting on the doorstep. Clara unfolded the parchment inside, reading the faded ink aloud: "The blood we gave was never enough. And now, it comes for yours."

The house seemed to shudder at the words, its walls straining as though they too felt the burden of the past. Edward clenched his fists. "It's warning us."

Silas, his voice low and edged with bitterness, muttered, "Or it's playing with us."

That night, Edward dreamed of chains dragging through empty halls, of spectral figures with hollow eyes and silent screams. When he awoke, he found himself in the library, the journal open to a page he had not seen before—an account of an ancient altar near the riverbend, a place where the first blood had been spilled to bind the land.

They made their way through the tangled woods at dawn, the cold seeping into their bones. At the riverbend, an ancient altar awaited, its stones darkened with age and something more sinister. As they approached, shadows stirred, coalescing into figures bound in chains, their faces twisted with sorrow and rage.

"Why have you come?" a voice hissed from the darkness.

"To end this," Edward replied, his voice steady.

"You cannot undo what has been done," the specter whispered. "Blood must pay for blood."

Clara's voice wavered. "Then take mine."

Silas's expression hardened. "Not all of us will leave this

place."

The altar pulsed with a dark energy, and Edward knew the time for silence was over. The past had come calling, and it would not be denied.

CHAPTER FORTY-ONE

D arlington House loomed like a spectral fortress against the ink-black sky, its silhouette fractured by flickering lightning that slashed through the dense, ominous clouds. The air inside carried an unnatural stillness, thick with the weight of memories too painful to name, and promises broken long before any of them had drawn breath. Every groan of the ancient timbers and flicker of the dim lanterns seemed like echoes of unseen eyes watching, waiting.

Edward Darlington sat in the library, hunched over an aged map spread across the mahogany desk, its corners weighted down by dusty tomes. His fingers traced the faded ink lines that marked the boundaries of the estate, but his mind was elsewhere—trapped in the tangled labyrinth of cursed history and blood debts that refused to die. The journal, with its crumbling pages filled with the agonized confessions of Thomas Darlington, lay open beside him.

Clara Langston stood by the window, the faint moonlight casting a silver sheen over her tired features. Her eyes, hollow from sleepless nights and restless thoughts, followed the winding path of the mist as it curled through the withered fields outside. Her voice trembled, breaking the suffocating silence. "Do you think they ever knew peace? The ones who came before us?"

Edward's voice was low, almost inaudible. "No. And neither will we if we fail."

A floorboard creaked, and Silas Boone emerged from the shadows of the doorway, his sharp gaze flickering between them. "We're not just fighting history," he said, his tone laced with sardonic dread. "We're fighting every sin our ancestors committed and every promise they broke."

Edward closed his eyes briefly, the weight of it all settling over him like a leaden shroud. "Then we need to know what the land wants."

A sudden, hollow knock reverberated through the house, each strike like a heartbeat too loud in the silence. Edward exchanged a glance with Clara before moving toward the door. When it creaked open, no one stood there. Only a single envelope, its parchment yellowed with age, lay waiting.

Clara unfolded the brittle paper, her voice shaking as she read aloud, "The blood we gave was never enough. And now, it comes for yours."

A shiver passed through them as if the house itself exhaled a long-held breath. Edward's jaw tightened. "It's not a warning. It's a demand."

Silas's smirk was humorless. "Then we better figure out what it wants before it takes it."

The night passed in fragmented whispers and restless shadows. Edward's dreams were a tapestry of sorrowful faces, chains dragging through darkened halls, and an ancient altar stained with blood. When he woke, the journal had opened to a page he did not recognize, detailing a forgotten room deep within the house—a room where Thomas Darlington had made his final promise.

They found the room at dawn, hidden behind a false panel in the library. Dust motes danced in the cold, stagnant air as Edward pried open a locked chest within. Inside, they found letters soaked in regret and a single locket with a portrait of Isolde Langston.

Clara's voice cracked. "This is where it started."

Edward's hand trembled as he lifted the locket. "And this is where it ends."

The past had come for them, and it would not be denied.

CHAPTER FORTY-TWO

The weight of unseen eyes pressed down upon Darlington House as the midnight hour crept closer, shrouding the estate in a darkness so profound it felt almost sentient. The house stood like a monument to forgotten sins, its weathered walls echoing with the silent screams of those who had come before. Lightning forked through the thick clouds, momentarily illuminating the gnarled trees whose roots clawed hungrily at the earth beneath.

Edward Darlington stood at the top of the grand staircase, the dim lantern in his hand casting trembling shadows along the corridor. His knuckles whitened as he gripped the banister, his eyes darting to the darkened corners where flickering shadows seemed to shift of their own accord. The faint whisper of voices, barely more than a breath, drifted through the still air, each syllable curling around him like unseen fingers.

Clara Langston's voice broke through the silence, soft but weighted with unease. "Something's waiting for us," she whispered, her breath forming a fragile mist in the cold air. She stood close, her dark eyes wide with unspoken fears, her presence the only anchor Edward clung to amidst the creeping dread.

From the far end of the hallway, Silas Boone emerged, his figure barely distinguishable from the shadows that seemed to cling to him. His sharp eyes, usually gleaming with mischievous defiance, now held a wary glint. "We've stirred something up," he muttered, his voice rough like gravel. "Something that doesn't want to be found."

Edward nodded, determination hardening his features. "Then we find it anyway."

The cellar door groaned as it swung open, revealing a narrow, spiraling staircase that plunged into the unknown. Each step echoed like a drumbeat, the air growing colder, thicker with every descent. The damp scent of earth and decay clung to them, a grim reminder that the past was never far beneath the surface.

Clara's lantern flickered violently as they reached the bottom, illuminating ancient stone walls entwined with roots that pulsed like veins. The whispers grew louder, swirling around them in a ghostly chorus. Edward's hand brushed against a crumbling wall, revealing symbols carved deeply into the stone—symbols of binding, of sacrifice, of promises never fulfilled.

"This is where it began," Clara whispered, her voice trembling like a fragile leaf.

A sudden, icy gust extinguished the lantern, plunging them into impenetrable darkness. The temperature plummeted, and spectral figures began to emerge, their faces twisted in agony, eyes hollow with unending despair.

A voice, ancient and filled with malice, echoed through the cellar. "You... cannot... escape..."

Silas's voice, though steady, held an edge of fear. "These are the forgotten souls... the ones buried beneath Darlington House."

Clara's hand gripped Edward's tightly. "They're the ones who paid the price."

Edward's voice was firm, though his heart pounded furiously. "Then we end this."

A distant, bone-chilling laugh echoed through the darkness, as the shadows pressed in closer.

The house wasn't haunted by its past. It was possessed by it.

CHAPTER FORTY-THREE

A low, mournful wail echoed through the very marrow of Darlington House, reverberating from the foundation to the rafters like a lament for sins too grievous to be forgotten. Edward Darlington's breath came in shallow gasps as he clutched the flickering lantern, its feeble glow barely holding back the creeping darkness that coiled around them like a serpent. Every creak of the ancient floorboards beneath his boots felt like a whisper from the unseen, each shadow an unwelcome guest that lingered just beyond sight.

Clara Langston stood beside him, her face pale, eyes wide with a blend of fear and determination. She clung to Edward's arm, her fingers trembling. "Do you hear that?" she whispered, her voice so soft it barely reached his ears.

Silas Boone, ever the cynic, forced a wry grin despite the tension that thickened the air around them. "Hard not to," he muttered. "Sounds like the dead finally got tired of whispering."

Yet, even his bravado couldn't mask the flicker of unease in his sharp eyes.

Suddenly, the floor beneath them shuddered violently, and a chilling gust of wind extinguished the lantern, plunging them into pitch-blackness. Edward's pulse quickened as he felt Clara's grip tighten. The house groaned, its timbers straining like ancient bones, and from beneath the floorboards came the unmistakable sound of chains dragging across wood.

A voice, distorted and broken, seeped through the cracks like a toxic mist. "You cannot run... you cannot hide..."

Clara gasped, her voice a fragile thread. "Who... who are you?"

The voice, ancient and malevolent, hissed, "We are the betrayed... the forgotten... the ones who scream beneath your feet."

Edward clenched his jaw, his voice steady despite the terror clawing at his chest. "What do you want from us?"

The response came like a chorus of tortured souls. "Vengeance."

Spectral figures began to materialize from the shadows —faces gaunt and hollow-eyed, their bodies bound in rusted chains that clanked with every movement. One figure, its face obscured by a bloodstained cloth, reached out with skeletal fingers.

Silas stepped back, his usual sarcasm failing him. "We need to move. Now."

But as Edward turned to flee, the floorboards cracked open beneath them, and ghostly hands reached through, clawing at their legs. Clara screamed, and Edward yanked her back, barely escaping the grasp of the spectral limbs.

"Let us go!" Edward bellowed, desperation lacing his voice.

A deafening scream erupted from beneath the floorboards, shaking the walls and rattling the very bones of the house. The lantern flickered back to life, illuminating the terror etched on their faces.

Edward's eyes blazed with resolve. "We need to finish this."

Clara nodded, her voice shaky but resolute. "Before they finish us."

The nightmare had only just begun.

CHAPTER FORTY-FOUR

The walls of Darlington House seemed to pulse with an ancient, malevolent energy, each timber steeped in the blood-soaked secrets of generations past. Edward Darlington stood motionless in the dim library, the flickering glow of the oil lamp casting restless shadows that stretched and recoiled with unnatural life. The weight of the journal in his hands felt heavier than ever, as though the words within were chains binding him to the sins of his forebears. His breath came slow and deliberate, but the storm of thoughts in his mind churned without rest.

Clara Langston, standing near the tall window, stared out into the endless night. Her reflection in the glass was ghostly, pale, and weary, but beyond her mirrored image, Edward thought he saw another figure—a spectral woman with hollow eyes and a silent, pleading mouth. Clara's voice broke the oppressive silence. "They know we're close," she whispered, her breath fogging the cold pane.

Silas Boone, perched on the edge of a faded armchair, his usual smirk absent, flicked the ash from a cigarette he hadn't yet lit. "Close to what? Salvation or damnation?" he muttered. His voice, usually laced with sarcasm, now carried the weight of a man who had stared into the abyss too long.

Before Edward could answer, the library door creaked open with agonizing slowness. The chill that filled the room was immediate and biting. In the doorway stood a young woman, her dress tattered, her wide eyes filled with sorrow and terror. She looked barely out of her teens, but her expression bore the weight of countless lifetimes.

"Who are you?" Clara asked, stepping forward cautiously.

The woman's voice trembled. "Lillian... I lived here once... long ago."

Edward swallowed hard. "Why have you come?"

"To warn you," she replied, her voice barely a whisper. "The curse... it runs deeper than you know. My family paid the first price. My father betrayed the land, and it took me."

Silas's eyes darkened. "And now it wants us?"

Lillian nodded solemnly. "It always wants more."

As the hours stretched on, Lillian's story unfolded like a nightmare given voice—a tale of forbidden love, betrayal, and a blood pact forged in desperation. Her spectral presence brought a new, haunting clarity to the curse's origins.

"How do we end it?" Clara's voice trembled with both fear and determination.

Lillian's gaze softened with sorrow. "Return what was taken."

Edward's heart pounded. "And what was that?"

"Innocence," Lillian whispered.

The revelation settled over them like a shroud.

The curse was no mere haunting. It was a legacy forged in blood.

CHAPTER FORTY-FIVE

The air inside Darlington House was thick with an unspoken dread, each shadow clinging to the walls as if reluctant to let go. Edward Darlington stood by the grand fireplace, the cold hearth mirroring the chill that gnawed at his soul. His fingers trembled as they clutched the weathered journal, its pages filled with his ancestor Thomas Darlington's desperate scrawl—a story of promises broken and blood spilled. The words weighed heavily on him, each sentence a link in the chain that bound him to the past.

Clara Langston sat nearby, her dark eyes reflecting the flickering light of a lantern. Her hands were clasped tightly in her lap, knuckles white from the strain. She met Edward's gaze, her voice barely a whisper. "What did you find?"

Edward's voice was grave, almost hollow. "It wasn't just blood they offered... it was trust. Trust they betrayed."

Silas Boone leaned against the doorframe, his smirk absent for once. "So what does that mean for us?"

Edward's jaw clenched. "It means the land won't rest until it takes what it was promised—and more."

The house groaned softly as if in agreement, and the three made their way to the cellar, each step echoing ominously. The descent into darkness felt endless, the weight of unseen eyes pressing down on them. The walls seemed to pulse with a life of their own, and when they reached the hidden chamber, the air grew thick with malevolence. An altar stood at the center, ancient symbols carved deep into its surface, glowing faintly.

"This is where it began," Clara whispered, her voice barely audible.

Before Edward could respond, the lantern's flame flickered violently before going out. Spectral figures emerged from the shadows, their hollow eyes fixed on the trio. A voice echoed through the chamber, low and menacing. "You carry the name... and the debt."

Edward's voice was steady despite his fear. "Then let me pay it."

Clara grabbed his arm, her voice sharp with panic. "No!"

The figure's response was chilling. "The price is not yours alone."

Edward's eyes widened in horror. "What does that mean?"

Silas's voice was grim. "It means none of us leaves unscathed."

The shadows surged forward, and the past reached for them with cold, unrelenting fingers.

The pact wasn't just forgotten. It was waiting.

CHAPTER FORTY-SIX

The silence that cloaked Darlington House had deepened into something almost sentient, as though the very walls held their breath in anticipation. Edward Darlington paced the dimly lit hallway, the lantern in his hand casting long, flickering shadows that seemed to stretch and coil with an unsettling life of their own. His mind was a tumult of thoughts, each one heavier than the last, burdened by the knowledge that the past was no longer content to remain buried.

Clara Langston followed closely, her footsteps nearly silent against the wooden floor. Her dark eyes scanned every corner, searching for something unseen yet undeniably present. She shivered as the cold seeped into her bones, whispering through the air like a warning. "Edward," she whispered, her voice barely audible, "they're watching us."

He nodded grimly, his jaw tight. "I know."

From the shadows at the far end of the hallway, Silas Boone emerged, his usual smirk replaced by a somber expression. "They've always been watching," he muttered, leaning against the wall. "But now... now they're waiting."

"Waiting for what?" Clara asked, her voice trembling.

Silas's eyes darkened. "For us to give them what they want."

The three gathered in the parlor, the air thick with unspoken fears and tension. Edward placed the journal on the table, its worn pages filled with secrets too dark to voice. Clara's voice was soft but resolute. "We need to understand them. If we don't, we'll never survive this."

Silas chuckled darkly, though there was no humor in his voice. "Understanding ghosts? Good luck with that."

Edward's gaze was sharp. "We don't have a choice."

"They were people once, Silas," Clara said gently. "People who were wronged."

Silas's eyes softened momentarily. "And now they're monsters."

A sudden chill swept through the room, extinguishing the lantern's flame. In the suffocating darkness, a whisper echoed, chilling them to the bone. "We were never monsters... until you made us."

Edward's breath caught. "Who's there?"

A faint glow illuminated the figure of a young woman —Lillian, the spectral figure they had encountered before. Her eyes shimmered with sorrow. "You cannot escape this," she whispered. "Not without paying the price."

Clara stepped forward, determination in her voice. "Tell us how to end it."

Lillian's voice trembled. "End it? You can't end what is bound by blood."

Edward's voice was barely above a whisper. "Then how do we break the chains?"

Lillian's gaze darkened. "By sacrificing what you love most."

Silas's eyes widened. "There has to be another way."

The shadows around them pulsed, and Lillian's figure flickered. "The land remembers," she whispered before vanishing.

Clara's voice broke the silence. "We have to try."

Edward nodded firmly. "Together."

The haunting wasn't over. It was only just beginning.

CHAPTER FORTY-SEVEN

A dense fog wrapped around Darlington House like a suffocating shroud, clinging to its weathered walls and seeping through the cracks. Edward Darlington stood at the window, watching as the mist curled through the skeletal branches of the ancient oaks, their gnarled limbs reaching toward the house as though in warning. His reflection in the glass appeared hollow, shadowed eyes staring back at him with an unfamiliar emptiness.

Clara Langston's voice, soft yet strained, broke the silence. "Edward... you haven't slept."

He turned to face her, the weight of sleepless nights evident in the tension lining his face. "I can't," he whispered. "Every time I close my eyes, they're there."

Clara nodded, understanding all too well. "The whispers... they're getting louder."

Silas Boone, leaning casually against the doorway despite the oppressive atmosphere, smirked without humor. "Louder?

They're screaming now."

Edward's gaze hardened. "We need answers."

The library felt colder than usual, the air heavy with an unseen presence. Clara traced her fingers along the spines of forgotten books, their leather bindings cracked with age.

"There has to be something here," she murmured, more to herself than to the others.

Silas snorted softly. "Because centuries of ghosts are going to leave us a how-to manual on breaking curses?"

Edward shot him a look. "Enough, Silas."

Clara's hand froze on a faded journal tucked behind a row of larger tomes. She pulled it free, dust swirling in the dim light. The name embossed on the cover made her breath hitch.

"Isolde Langston," she whispered.

Edward's heart pounded. "The woman Thomas Darlington loved."

As Clara opened the journal, a cold breeze swept through the room, extinguishing the lantern's flame. The darkness pressed in, but not before a whisper, faint and sorrowful, filled the air.

"I was never meant to be forgotten..."

Edward lit the lantern again, his hands trembling. "She's here."

Clara read aloud, her voice steady despite the chill that gnawed at her bones. "'Our love was our sin, and our punishment eternal. I was the price he paid, and my soul... bound to this land.'"

Silas's voice was barely a whisper. "She was the sacrifice."

A sudden knock echoed through the room, though no one stood at the door. Edward's breath hitched. "They're not going to let us leave."

Clara's eyes, wide and fearful, met his. "Then we fight."

The house groaned, its ancient timbers straining under an unseen weight.

The past wasn't ready to let go.

rn in his hand casting long, flickering shadows that seemed to stretch and coil with an unsettling life of their own. His mind was a tumult of thoughts, each one heavier than the last, burdened by the knowledge that the past was no longer content to remain buried.

Clara Langston followed closely, her footsteps nearly silent against the wooden floor. Her dark eyes scanned every corner, searching for something unseen yet undeniably present. She shivered as the cold seeped into her bones, whispering through the air like a warning. "Edward," she whispered, her voice barely audible, "they're watching us."

He nodded grimly, his jaw tight. "I know."

From the shadows at the far end of the hallway, Silas Boone emerged, his usual smirk replaced by a somber expression. "They've always been watching," he muttered, leaning against the wall. "But now... now they're waiting."

"Waiting for what?" Clara asked, her voice trembling.

Silas's eyes darkened. "For us to give them what they want."

The three gathered in the parlor, the air thick with

unspoken fears and tension. Edward placed the journal on the table, its worn pages filled with secrets too dark to voice. Clara's voice was soft but resolute. "We need to understand them. If we don't, we'll never survive this."

Silas chuckled darkly, though there was no humor in his voice. "Understanding ghosts? Good luck with that."

Edward's gaze was sharp. "We don't have a choice."

"They were people once, Silas," Clara said gently. "People who were wronged."

Silas's eyes softened momentarily. "And now they're monsters."

A sudden chill swept through the room, extinguishing the lantern's flame. In the suffocating darkness, a whisper echoed, chilling them to the bone. "We were never monsters... until you made us."

Edward's breath caught. "Who's there?"

A faint glow illuminated the figure of a young woman —Lillian, the spectral figure they had encountered before. Her eyes shimmered with sorrow. "You cannot escape this," she whispered. "Not without paying the price."

Clara stepped forward, determination in her voice. "Tell us how to end it."

Lillian's voice trembled. "End it? You can't end what is bound by blood."

Edward's voice was barely above a whisper. "Then how do we break the chains?"

Lillian's gaze darkened. "By sacrificing what you love most."

Silas's eyes widened. "There has to be another way."

The shadows around them pulsed, and Lillian's figure flickered. "The land remembers," she whispered before vanishing.

Clara's voice broke the silence. "We have to try."

Edward nodded firmly. "Together."

The haunting wasn't over. It was only just beginning.

CHAPTER FORTY-EIGHT

The fog wove its way around Darlington House like a spectral tapestry, its icy fingers tracing every windowpane and seeping into the very foundation of the ancient estate. Edward Darlington stood at the window, his breath fogging the glass as he peered into the mist, where the skeletal branches of ancient oaks swayed like mournful sentinels. The weight of sleepless nights pulled at his shoulders, his reflection in the glass hollow-eyed and gaunt, a stark mirror to the turmoil within.

Clara Langston's soft voice pierced the oppressive silence, filled with quiet concern. "Edward... you haven't slept," she whispered, standing in the doorway wrapped in a thick shawl, her dark eyes reflecting both exhaustion and a tender worry that stirred something deep within him.

He turned slowly, the flickering lantern casting shadows that danced across the room. "I can't," he replied, voice strained and fragile. "Every time I close my eyes, they're there. Watching.

Whispering."

Clara stepped closer, her hand grazing the edge of the desk, steadying herself. "The whispers," she breathed, almost afraid to say it aloud, "they're getting louder, aren't they?"

From the doorway, Silas Boone's sharp silhouette cut through the dim light, his usual smirk absent, replaced by an unspoken unease. "Louder? They're screaming now," he muttered, crossing his arms as if trying to shield himself from the unseen eyes he felt upon him.

Edward's jaw tightened. "We need answers. Now more than ever."

The library enveloped them in an unsettling hush, every corner steeped in an ancient stillness that pressed against their chests. Clara traced her fingertips along the spines of forgotten tomes, the dust swirling around her touch as if stirred from centuries-long slumber.

"There has to be something here," she whispered, more to herself than to the others, her voice almost lost to the room's oppressive silence.

Silas's chuckle was bitter, devoid of humor. "Sure. I'm sure there's a guidebook titled 'How to Break a Centuries-Old Blood Curse' lying around here somewhere."

Edward's glare silenced him. "Not now, Silas."

Clara's hand paused on a slim, worn journal hidden behind larger, more imposing volumes. She slid it out carefully, heart pounding as she read the embossed name on the cover. "Isolde Langston," she whispered, her voice trembling.

Edward's pulse quickened. "The woman Thomas Darlington loved."

Clara opened the journal with reverence, her eyes scanning the faded script as an icy breeze swept through the room, snuffing out the lantern and plunging them into a darkness thick with unseen presence. A sorrowful whisper echoed around them, sending shivers down their spines.

"I was never meant to be forgotten..."

Edward relit the lantern with shaky hands, the flame illuminating their pale faces. "She's here."

Clara's voice quivered as she read, "'Our love was our sin, and our punishment eternal. I was the price he paid, and my soul... bound to this land.'"

Silas's voice was barely a whisper. "She was the sacrifice."

A rhythmic knock echoed through the room, loud and deliberate, though the doorway remained empty.

Edward's breath quickened. "They're not going to let us leave."

Clara's wide, fearful eyes met his, determination flickering within them. "Then we fight."

The house groaned in response, its ancient timbers creaking under the weight of secrets too long buried.

The past wasn't ready to let go—and neither were they.

CHAPTER FORTY-NINE

The fog wrapped around Darlington House like a living shroud, curling through the withered branches of ancient oaks and clinging to the estate's timeworn façade. Edward Darlington stood at the window, his reflection ghostly in the glass, hollow-eyed and gaunt from sleepless nights. The weight of centuries-old secrets pressed on his chest, making each breath feel labored. Outside, the mist seemed alive, whispering promises of torment and truths yet unrevealed.

Clara Langston's soft voice, thick with worry, broke the silence. "Edward... you haven't slept," she whispered, stepping into the room. Wrapped in a shawl, her dark eyes shimmered with both exhaustion and unspoken concern.

He turned slowly, the lantern's flame flickering in his grasp. "I can't," he whispered hoarsely. "Every time I close my eyes, they're there—watching, waiting."

Clara moved closer, her fingers brushing the desk's edge for balance. "The whispers... they're louder now, aren't they?"

From the doorway, Silas Boone's silhouette cut through the dim light, his usual sarcasm replaced by grim unease. "Louder? They're practically screaming." His voice was tight, betraying the fear he rarely showed.

Edward's expression hardened. "We need answers. Now."

The library, a fortress of forgotten knowledge, swallowed their whispers, its shadows thick and watchful. Clara's fingertips grazed the spines of ancient tomes, dust swirling like disturbed memories. "There must be something here," she murmured.

Silas snorted. "Sure, maybe there's a 'How to Break a Centuries-Old Curse' manual tucked behind the grimoires."

"Enough, Silas," Edward snapped.

Clara's hand trembled as she pulled a slim, aged journal from its hiding place. The name embossed on the cover made her breath hitch. "Isolde Langston."

Edward's pulse quickened. "The woman Thomas Darlington loved."

She opened the journal, her voice hushed. "'Our love was our sin, our punishment eternal. I was the price he paid, my soul bound to this land.'"

A cold wind extinguished the lantern, and a sorrowful whisper filled the room. "I was never meant to be forgotten..."

Edward relit the flame, illuminating pale faces. "She's here."

Silas's voice, barely a whisper, trembled. "She was the sacrifice."

A knock, rhythmic and deliberate, echoed through the room though the doorway remained empty.

Edward's breath quickened. "They're not going to let us leave."

Clara's wide, fearful eyes locked onto his, determination flickering beneath her fear. "Then we fight."

The house groaned, its ancient bones creaking under the weight of secrets too long buried.

The past wasn't ready to let go—and neither were they.

CHAPTER FIFTY

T he fog that coiled around Darlington House that night felt sentient, as if it were not merely a trick of the weather but a living thing, ancient and malicious, draping itself over the estate like a suffocating shroud. Edward Darlington stood at the edge of the parlor window, his reflection flickering in the fragile glow of the lantern beside him. The glass distorted his features—hollow eyes rimmed with sleeplessness, the sharp angles of his face carved deeper by worry—and for a fleeting moment, he thought he saw another face, spectral and familiar, staring back.

"Edward..." Clara Langston's voice, soft but laced with apprehension, floated through the stillness. She stood at the doorway, her shawl draped loosely over her shoulders, dark curls spilling down her back, and eyes clouded with exhaustion. "You haven't slept."

He turned slowly, the lantern's flame casting dancing shadows across his face. "I can't," he admitted, voice raw with fatigue. "Every time I close my eyes, I feel them... watching... waiting."

Clara crossed the room with careful steps, her hand brushing the edge of the desk as if grounding herself. "The whispers... they're louder now, aren't they?"

A figure leaned casually in the doorway, though the tension in his frame betrayed his nonchalance. Silas Boone's usual sardonic expression had darkened into something far more serious. "Louder?" he muttered. "They're screaming bloody murder." His smirk faltered, and for once, fear flickered in his sharp gaze.

Edward's jaw tightened, and he exhaled sharply. "We need answers. Now."

The library, once a haven of knowledge, now felt like a trap, its towering shelves and shadowed corners watching them as intently as the unseen forces that lurked within the walls. Clara's fingers skimmed the spines of ancient tomes, each title a whispered promise or a forgotten curse, as dust swirled in their wake. "There has to be something here," she murmured, voice barely audible.

Silas chuckled darkly, though it lacked his usual bravado. "Sure. Maybe there's a 'Breaking Curses for Dummies' tucked behind these relics."

"Silas," Edward snapped, his voice cutting through the tension.

Clara's breath hitched as she tugged a slim, worn journal from behind a row of crumbling books. The name embossed on its cover made her hand tremble. "Isolde Langston."

Edward's breath caught. "The woman Thomas Darlington loved."

She opened the journal, her voice soft, reverent. "'Our

love was our sin, our punishment eternal. I was the price he paid, my soul bound to this land.'"

A chill swept through the room, extinguishing the lantern's flame. In the darkness, a voice whispered, sorrowful and distant. "I was never meant to be forgotten..."

Edward relit the lantern, its glow revealing faint outlines of faces, pale and mournful, watching them.

"She's here," Edward whispered.

Silas's voice trembled, barely audible. "She was the sacrifice."

A sudden knock echoed through the room, rhythmic and deliberate, though the doorway remained empty. The sound reverberated through their bones.

Edward's voice was steady, though his hands clenched into fists. "They're not going to let us leave."

Clara met his gaze, fear and determination swirling in her dark eyes. "Then we fight."

The house groaned, its ancient timbers straining under the weight of secrets too long buried. The past wasn't ready to let go.

But neither were they.

CHAPTER FIFTY-ONE

The fog outside Darlington House had thickened into an impenetrable wall, swallowing the grounds in silence, but within the house, the air crackled with unseen tension, thick and suffocating. Edward Darlington sat at the grand oak table in the library, his hands gripping the edges as though the weight of his thoughts alone might crush him. The journal lay open before him, its pages fragile with age yet burdened with revelations too heavy to bear. His eyes, shadowed by sleepless nights, scanned the words over and over, but no clarity came.

Clara Langston stood behind him, her arms wrapped around herself, eyes gleaming with both exhaustion and determination. She watched Edward with a quiet intensity, her voice barely a murmur in the stillness. "We've come too far to turn back now, Edward. But... do you ever wonder if it's already too late?"

Edward's jaw clenched, his voice a rough whisper. "If it is... then we never had a chance to begin with."

A scoff came from the doorway. Silas Boone, his signature

smirk replaced by a grim frown, leaned against the frame with crossed arms. "Cheerful thought. So, what's the plan now? Spill some blood, whisper an apology to the restless dead, and hope they're in a forgiving mood?" His tone was sharp, but his eyes betrayed the fear he dared not voice.

Edward's gaze remained steady. "We find the altar. We end this."

The cellar awaited them, its narrow staircase descending into an abyss of darkness that seemed alive. Each step down felt like an unspoken pact, the air growing colder with each breath they took. Clara's lantern flickered, casting hesitant light against the stone walls, illuminating symbols carved with shaking hands centuries before.

"This place..." Clara whispered, her voice trembling as her eyes locked on the altar ahead, worn and cracked from forgotten rituals. "This is where it began."

A whisper filled the air, sorrowful and laced with pain. "And where it must end."

They turned to see Isolde Langston's spectral figure, her form shimmering faintly, eyes hollow with centuries of sorrow.

"Isolde..." Clara breathed. "Tell us how to end this."

The ghost's voice wavered. "The land must be satisfied. A soul bound willingly."

Edward's voice was a choked whisper. "There has to be another way."

Isolde's form flickered. "There isn't."

Silas's usual sarcasm was gone, replaced by a grim reality. "So, who's going to pay the price?"

The silence that followed was deafening.

The altar awaited its final sacrifice.

And the house would not be denied.

CHAPTER FIFTY-TWO

The fog outside Darlington House clung to the night like an omen, its thick tendrils pressing against the windows, curling around the ancient trees like spectral fingers. Inside, the house breathed with an unsettling stillness, its walls vibrating with unseen tension. Edward Darlington stood motionless in the library, his breath shallow as he stared at the flickering candle on the table. The journal lay open before him, its faded ink a grim reminder of promises broken and debts unpaid.

Clara Langston sat across from him, her eyes reflecting the weight of their shared burden. "Edward... what if we don't make it through this?" she whispered, her voice fragile but steady.

His gaze softened, and he reached for her hand. "Then we face it together."

A sharp laugh from the doorway broke the moment. Silas Boone, ever the cynic, leaned against the frame with arms crossed. "Together or not, this house isn't going to let us waltz out alive without a fight."

Edward nodded grimly. "Then let's give it one."

The cellar door creaked open, revealing the narrow staircase that spiraled into darkness. Each step felt like a descent into something ancient and unforgiving. The air grew colder, more oppressive, as they moved deeper into the bowels of the house. Clara's lantern flickered violently, casting jittery shadows along the stone walls carved with symbols etched by desperate hands long ago.

"This place... it feels wrong," Clara murmured, her voice barely audible.

Edward's jaw tightened. "Because it is."

The chamber at the bottom was larger than they remembered, the altar now pulsing with a sinister energy that made the air hum. The stone surface bore dark stains that whispered of past sacrifices.

Silas took a step back. "Yeah, this place is definitely trying to kill us."

Suddenly, the shadows twisted and stretched, forming the spectral figures of those bound to the land. Isolde Langston materialized at the forefront, her sorrowful eyes locking onto Edward's.

"The blood must flow," she whispered. "There is no other way."

Edward's breath caught. "Then take mine."

Clara gasped. "No!"

Isolde's form flickered. "It is not yours alone. The land demands balance."

A deep rumble shook the room as ghostly chains erupted

from the walls, binding Edward, Clara, and Silas in place.

Silas struggled. "I knew this would end badly."

Edward's voice was determined. "We end this tonight."

The altar awaited its sacrifice.

And the house would not be denied.

CHAPTER FIFTY-THREE

The fog outside Darlington House thickened into an impenetrable veil, as if the night itself sought to conceal what was to come. Inside, the house seemed to pulse with a malevolent awareness, each groan of its ancient timbers a whispered threat. Edward Darlington stood in the dim glow of a single lantern, its flickering flame barely illuminating the oppressive darkness around him. The weight of the past pressed heavily on his shoulders, each revelation from the cursed journal carving deeper into his soul.

Clara Langston hovered nearby, her dark eyes clouded with dread and determination. She clutched the journal tightly against her chest, its brittle pages filled with secrets too monstrous to comprehend. "Edward," she whispered, her voice a fragile thread, "I feel it watching us."

Edward nodded, his jaw clenched. "It's always watching."

Silas Boone, ever the cynic, leaned casually against the doorway, though the tension in his eyes betrayed his unease.

"Then let's not keep it waiting."

The trio descended into the cellar, the narrow staircase winding like a serpent into the bowels of the house. Each step was a descent into forgotten horrors. The walls, slick with damp, seemed to close in, their surfaces etched with symbols that pulsed faintly, as if alive. Clara's lantern quivered violently, casting erratic shadows that twisted into grotesque shapes.

"This place..." Clara's voice faltered. "It feels wrong."

Edward's response was grim. "Because it is."

The chamber at the bottom stretched endlessly, the ancient altar at its center bathed in an eerie glow. Its surface, worn smooth by centuries of blood, seemed to hum with anticipation. The shadows thickened, coalescing into spectral figures whose hollow eyes bore into their souls.

Isolde Langston's ghostly form appeared, her sorrow palpable. "The blood must flow," she intoned.

Edward's voice broke the silence. "Then take mine."

Clara's heart clenched. "No!"

Isolde's eyes softened. "It is not yours alone. The land demands balance."

Chains erupted from the walls, binding them in place. Silas gritted his teeth. "Knew this would end badly."

Edward's voice, though strained, held firm resolve. "We end this tonight."

The altar awaited its sacrifice. And the house would not be denied.

CHAPTER FIFTY-FOUR

The fog outside Darlington House clung to the skeletal branches of ancient oaks like the fingers of forgotten souls, weaving a veil of impenetrable dread over the crumbling estate. The house, long decayed by time and secrets, seemed to inhale the thick mist, its windows flickering with unseen memories. Inside, the air grew heavier with each passing moment, dense with the whispers of those long gone, their unseen eyes watching.

Edward Darlington stood at the top of the cellar staircase, his grip firm on the lantern that sputtered weakly, its dim light reluctant to pierce the oppressive darkness below. Every heartbeat felt like a countdown, every shallow breath a reminder of the weight he bore—not just for himself, but for generations past. The sins of his ancestors clawed at him, unseen but ever-present.

Behind him, Clara Langston clutched the cursed journal to her chest, its fragile pages filled with the ink of blood and betrayal. Her dark eyes shimmered with both fear and determination, a fragile balance teetering on the edge of despair. "Edward," she whispered, her voice barely a tremor against the suffocating silence, "it knows we're coming."

He turned to her, his expression a mixture of resolve and tenderness, the kind that spoke of shared burdens and unspoken promises. "Then let it know we're ready," he replied softly.

A scoff echoed from behind them. Silas Boone leaned against the wall, his smirk barely concealing the unease flickering in his sharp eyes. "Ready to do what, exactly? Offer ourselves up like lambs to the slaughter?"

"Survive," Edward shot back, his voice cutting through the tension like a blade. Without waiting for a retort, he stepped forward, leading them down the narrow, spiraling staircase into the abyss.

The walls of the staircase, slick with moisture that had seeped through centuries of stone, whispered as they descended. Ancient symbols, carved deep into the walls, glimmered faintly under the flickering lantern light, each one a haunting reminder of the dark rituals that bound the Darlington and Langston bloodlines to a curse older than memory itself. Clara's hand tightened around Edward's arm, her breath shallow.

"This place... it feels alive," she murmured, her voice barely audible.

Edward's jaw clenched. "Because it is."

The staircase ended abruptly, opening into a cavernous chamber hewn from the earth itself. The ancient blood altar stood at the center, its surface darkened by generations of sacrifice, a grotesque monument to the unquenchable hunger of the land. The air vibrated with unseen energy, a low hum that resonated through their bones, and the shadows along the walls twisted unnaturally, stretching and contorting as if welcoming them.

Clara's lantern flickered violently, casting grotesque shapes that seemed to mock their presence. From the darkness, spectral figures began to emerge, their hollow eyes glistening with unending torment. Among them, Isolde Langston's ethereal form materialized, her sorrowful gaze cutting through the tension like a cold blade.

"The blood must flow," she intoned, her voice a haunting echo of centuries past, layered with anguish and regret.

Edward stepped forward, his heart pounding but his voice steady. "Then take mine," he offered, each word a sacrifice of its own.

"No!" Clara's voice cracked, her desperation palpable as she reached for him. Tears welled in her eyes, but Isolde's ghostly presence held her in place.

Isolde's spectral gaze softened, the weight of her own sorrow evident. "It is not yours alone. The land demands balance."

Suddenly, chains of spectral light erupted from the walls, binding Edward, Clara, and Silas in place. Silas, gritting his teeth, struggled futilely against the bonds. "I swear," he muttered, half in jest and half in resignation, "if we die down here, I'm haunting both of you."

Edward's hand trembled as it pressed against the cold altar, the stone pulsing under his touch as if alive. Clara's tears fell freely, mingling with the droplets of blood drawn from Edward's palm. The ancient symbols carved into the altar began to glow, and the very walls of Darlington House shuddered in response.

The house screamed, its anguished wail reverberating through the walls and into the night beyond. The altar waited, patient and insatiable. The past, unrelenting, would have its vengeance.

CHAPTER FIFTY-FIVE

The darkness within Darlington House was more than the absence of light—it was a living, breathing entity that clung to every surface, whispering promises of doom. Edward Darlington moved through the dim hallway with deliberate, cautious steps, each footfall a soft echo that seemed to stretch endlessly through the oppressive silence. The flickering lantern in his hand wavered, its feeble flame casting quivering shadows that danced and distorted along the cracked wallpaper, mirroring the turmoil in Edward's mind.

Behind him, Clara Langston followed closely, her breath shallow, her fingers brushing the cold, crumbling walls as if anchoring herself to something tangible amidst the intangible dread. "Edward," she whispered, her voice barely audible, "it's... watching us." Her wide, fear-laden eyes darted into the shadows that seemed to shift and swell around them.

Edward's jaw tightened, his voice a low murmur. "It always is." The weight of the house's unseen gaze pressed down on him like a shroud.

From the end of the corridor, Silas Boone's voice,

usually edged with dry sarcasm, was grim. "I don't think it's just watching anymore." His sharp eyes, so often alight with mischief, were now narrowed with a somber intensity.

Suddenly, a door creaked open on its own, revealing a narrow staircase that spiraled downward into darkness, an invitation laced with menace.

"Great," Silas muttered, forcing a humorless smirk. "Because basements always go well in haunted houses."

Edward shot him a sharp glance, but Clara's hand on his arm calmed him. Her touch, though trembling, was steady with resolve. "We have to go," she said softly, her voice carrying an unspoken plea.

The descent was slow, each step accompanied by the unsettling creak of aged wood under their weight. The air grew colder, sharper, carrying the faint, acrid scent of burnt wood and something metallic—something unmistakably like blood. The shadows thickened, pressing closer, as if urging them back.

At the bottom, they found themselves in a large, cavernous chamber, the walls blackened with soot and covered in ancient symbols carved deep into the stone—sigils of binding, of sacrifice. In the center stood a charred altar, its surface marred by centuries of blood offerings, the ash clinging to it like a shroud.

Clara's voice cracked, barely a whisper. "This place... it's where it happened." Her hand trembled as she reached out, but she pulled back, unable to touch the altar's cold surface.

Edward swallowed hard, his voice thick. "Where they made the first sacrifice."

From the shadows, a voice hissed—low, guttural, and

ancient. "And where the last must be made."

Clara gasped as ghostly figures emerged—spectral forms with hollow eyes and outstretched hands. One figure stepped forward, its face obscured by a veil of ash, its voice a whisper against the cold air. "The blood of the innocent sealed the pact. The blood of the guilty must break it."

Silas frowned, his voice sharp with bitter disbelief. "And who's guilty?"

The spirit's eyes, voids of darkness, locked onto them. "You are all guilty."

Edward's heart pounded violently in his chest. "Then let's end it."

The chamber trembled, the very walls seeming to pulse with malevolent energy as the spirits closed in.

The house demanded retribution. And it would not be denied.

CHAPTER FIFTY-SIX

T he oppressive weight of Darlington House bore down upon Edward Darlington as he stood in the grand hall, its towering ceilings lost in shadow. The ancient walls whispered incessantly, an eerie murmur threading through the silence, each indistinct voice a remnant of a soul long trapped within the cursed foundations. His breath came shallow and strained, carrying the sharp tang of old wood, damp stone, and something far more sinister—something metallic, almost like blood.

Clara Langston's soft footsteps echoed behind him, her presence a fragile tether to sanity in this waking nightmare. Her fingers, delicate but trembling, trailed along the banister's dust-coated surface until she reached Edward's side. Her whisper was barely audible but resolute. "It's close... I can feel it."

Edward's jaw clenched tightly, his voice low and steady. "So can I."

From the shadows, Silas Boone emerged, his dark eyes sharp and unreadable. His usual sardonic grin was absent, replaced by a grim determination. "Then let's hope it doesn't feel us first."

They moved down a corridor that seemed to stretch endlessly, the flickering lantern casting wavering shadows along the peeling wallpaper. Each step resonated like a drumbeat, each breath a shallow gasp against the thick, suffocating air. Clara's fingers tightened around Edward's arm. "Do you hear that?" she whispered.

A faint, rhythmic tapping echoed from behind the walls, like skeletal fingers drumming against the wooden panels. Edward swallowed hard, his pulse quickening. "It knows we're here."

Without warning, the wall beside them buckled, and a ghastly hand shot out—skeletal and covered in decaying flesh. Clara screamed, stumbling back into Edward's arms. Silas cursed under his breath, pulling them away as more hands reached from the walls, grasping at empty air.

"Run!" Edward shouted, dragging Clara down the hall.

They burst into the dining hall, where a long table was still set with tarnished silverware and dust-covered plates. The chandelier flickered ominously overhead. Clara, panting and wide-eyed, gasped, "We can't keep running."

Edward nodded firmly. "We face it."

The air grew colder, and Thomas Darlington's spectral figure materialized at the head of the table, his hollow eyes filled with sorrow. "The pact cannot be undone," he whispered. "Blood must pay the price."

Silas stepped forward, his voice steady despite the terror in his eyes. "Then take mine."

"No!" Clara's voice cracked with desperation.

Edward's eyes darkened with determination. "We choose who pays."

The house trembled, its foundations groaning under the weight of past sins. The choice loomed over them, heavy and unforgiving.

The past's grip tightened. And the price would be paid.

CHAPTER FIFTY-SEVEN

The air in Darlington House clung like an icy shroud, thick with the weight of unseen eyes. Edward Darlington's every step echoed through the grand hall, each footfall a whisper against the ancient wood. The lantern in his hand sputtered, casting long, wavering shadows that seemed to stretch toward him, grasping and restless. His face, drawn and weary, betrayed the torment that clawed at his mind, each heartbeat a painful reminder of the past he could no longer escape.

Beside him, Clara Langston's fingers tightened around his arm, her breaths shallow and uneven. Her dark eyes, wide with fear and determination, darted across the corridor, searching the gloom. "Edward," she whispered, voice trembling like the flickering flame, "it's waiting."

Edward's jaw tightened, a grim resolve settling in his chest. "Then let it wait. We end this tonight."

Silas Boone's figure emerged from the shadows, his usual

sardonic smirk absent. His eyes, sharp and calculating, held a rare seriousness. "End it? It's not going to let us walk away without a fight."

They moved with cautious determination, each creak of the floorboards beneath their feet a harbinger of the horrors lurking within the walls. The silence was broken only by the faint sound of rhythmic tapping—like skeletal fingers drumming against unseen surfaces.

"Do you hear that?" Clara whispered, her voice barely audible.

Edward nodded, muscles tense. "They're restless."

Silas let out a humorless chuckle. "Restless? They're furious."

The cellar door groaned open before them, revealing the abyss beyond. As they descended the narrow staircase, the air grew sharper, biting at their skin with each step. The altar loomed in the shadows, its ancient symbols glowing faintly like veins pulsing with dark energy. Clara shuddered, her voice cracking, "This is where it ends."

From the darkness, Thomas Darlington's spectral figure materialized, his hollow eyes locking onto Edward's. "The pact cannot be undone," he whispered. "Blood must pay the price."

Silas stepped forward, voice steady despite the terror flickering in his eyes. "Then take mine."

Clara's voice broke with desperation. "No!"

Edward's gaze darkened with fierce determination. "We choose who pays."

The house trembled violently, its ancient bones groaning.

The choice hung heavy in the air, the weight of centuries pressing down upon them.

The past's grip tightened, and the shadows held their breath, waiting for the price to be paid.

CHAPTER FIFTY-EIGHT

The suffocating stillness within Darlington House felt almost unbearable, as though the very walls strained under the weight of countless unspoken horrors. Edward Darlington's breath came in shallow, uneven bursts as he stood before the altar, its surface cold beneath his fingertips. The flickering lantern cast long shadows that danced ominously along the stone walls, each movement a silent reminder that time was running out.

Clara Langston's voice, though barely a whisper, sliced through the silence. "Edward... I can't lose you."

He turned to her, his eyes dark with resolve but softened by the fear he couldn't hide. "We don't have a choice, Clara. The house—this curse—it won't stop until it takes what it's owed."

From the far corner, Silas Boone leaned against the wall, his face shadowed but his voice steady. "Then let's make sure it takes the right thing."

The air grew colder, sharp as a blade against their

skin, as spectral figures began to materialize around them —ghostly remnants of the past, their hollow eyes reflecting centuries of agony. Edward's heart pounded violently as Thomas Darlington's apparition emerged, his expression both sorrowful and unrelenting.

"The pact was never meant to be broken," Thomas whispered, his voice echoing through the chamber. "But it can be transferred."

Clara's eyes widened. "Transferred? To who?"

Thomas's gaze locked onto Edward. "To him. To me. To any who bear the name."

Edward's voice cracked. "I'll do it."

Clara stepped forward, tears streaming down her face. "No! There has to be another way."

Silas's smirk was grim. "There's always another way. We just have to find it before the house finds us."

The walls trembled, and the altar pulsed with a dark energy. A voice, ancient and unyielding, filled the room. "Choose, or we choose for you."

Edward clenched his fists. "We end this tonight."

Clara's voice trembled. "But at what cost?"

The spirits surged forward, and the choice loomed closer.

The pact demanded its due. And the night was far from over.

CHAPTER FIFTY-NINE

The silence that stretched through Darlington House no longer felt like mere emptiness; it was an oppressive force, thick with dread and steeped in the memories of generations long gone. Edward Darlington stood rigid before the altar, the weight of the past pressing down on him like a millstone. His fingers trembled over the ancient carvings etched into the cold stone, each groove a silent testament to the sacrifices made before him. The flickering lantern in his grip cast erratic shadows across the chamber walls, creating twisted figures that seemed to reach for him from the darkness.

Clara Langston's soft, strained whisper shattered the fragile stillness. "Edward... there has to be another way. Please." Her voice cracked under the strain, her eyes shimmering with unshed tears, pleading with him not to do what they both feared.

Edward turned to her, the turmoil in his chest mirrored in the storm behind his dark gaze. "If there is another way, Clara, we haven't found it yet. And time is running out." His voice was steady, but the tremor in his hands betrayed his fear.

From the shadows, Silas Boone's grim chuckle echoed faintly. "We're past hoping for miracles, Darlington. If we don't make a move, the house will make it for us—and trust me, we won't like its choice." His usual sarcasm was gone, replaced by a harsh realism that hung heavily in the air.

The ghostly figure of Thomas Darlington materialized beside the altar, his spectral form shimmering like mist in the flickering lantern light. His hollow eyes, void of warmth, locked onto Edward. "The pact cannot be undone without sacrifice," Thomas intoned, his voice cold as the grave. "One of you must stay."

Clara's breath hitched painfully, her tears now streaming freely down her cheeks. "No! There has to be another way!" Her voice, though desperate, carried a fierce resolve.

Edward's fists clenched tightly at his sides. "Then tell us how, Thomas. Tell us how to break this curse without blood."

Thomas's gaze remained unwavering. "There is no breaking the curse... only transferring it."

Silas stepped forward, his tone sharp and dry. "And who gets to wear the chain this time?"

Thomas's hollow eyes shifted to Clara. "The bloodline must remain," he whispered.

Edward's voice broke, raw with emotion. "No. I won't let that happen."

Clara's tear-filled eyes met Edward's, her voice a fragile whisper. "Then who, Edward? Who will it take?"

The walls around them shuddered, the carved symbols glowing faintly as if stirred by their anguish. A deep, ancient voice reverberated through the chamber, cold and unrelenting.

"Choose... or be chosen."

Silas's smirk returned, but it was bitter. "Guess this is where we find out who's really willing to bleed for this place."

Edward's breath came faster, his heart pounding like a drum in his chest. "No one has to die."

Thomas's whisper sliced through the room like a knife. "But someone must stay."

Clara's hand trembled as she reached for Edward's, her voice barely audible. "Together."

Edward nodded, his reply a whisper lost to the darkness. "Together."

The shadows pulsed violently, spectral hands reaching out as the final choice loomed over them.

The past's grip tightened. And the final price would be paid.

CHAPTER SIXTY

The silence in Darlington House was shattered by Edward Darlington's anguished cry as Clara Langston's form dissolved into the shadows before him, her final whisper lingering like a faint echo in the suffocating stillness: "I'm still here..." Those three words, fragile yet haunting, twisted like a dagger in his chest, the weight of her sacrifice pressing down on him with unbearable finality. He stumbled back from the altar, the ancient carvings now glowing faintly with the energy of the pact sealed by Clara's soul. His heart pounded violently, each beat resonating like a funeral drum through the vast chamber.

Silas Boone groaned as he pushed himself up from where he had been thrown against the stone wall, pain etched into his usually sharp features. His dark eyes, often filled with sardonic wit, now brimmed with raw disbelief and sorrow. "She can't be gone," Edward whispered, his voice barely audible and breaking under the weight of his grief. His hands clenched into fists, trembling. "She can't..."

Silas, approaching cautiously, placed a steadying hand on Edward's shoulder, his usual bravado stripped away, leaving only bare honesty. "Edward... the curse... it took her." His voice cracked at the last word, the reality too harsh even for him.

Edward turned sharply, eyes blazing with desperate determination. "No. There has to be a way to bring her back. There has to be." His voice, though strong, quivered with the anguish that rippled through every fiber of his being.

The temperature plummeted, and Thomas Darlington's spectral form flickered back into existence, his expression a mixture of sorrow and resignation. "The pact is sealed," Thomas intoned solemnly. "Her soul is bound to the house now."

Edward's fists slammed onto the altar, the sound echoing through the chamber. "Then I'll break it," he hissed through clenched teeth. "I'll tear this place apart brick by brick if I have to."

Thomas's hollow gaze softened. "You cannot," he whispered. "The house is no longer just a place—it's an entity, an ancient hunger that feeds on sacrifice."

Silas's voice, usually dripping with sarcasm, was tight with frustration. "So what? We just leave? Let Clara suffer forever?"

A faint shimmer flickered near the altar, and Clara's ethereal form appeared, her eyes shimmering with unshed tears and unwavering love. "Edward..." she whispered, her voice soft as a breeze yet cutting through the darkness with haunting clarity.

Edward lunged forward instinctively, reaching out, but his hands passed through her translucent figure. "Clara," he choked, tears streaming down his face, "I'll find a way to save you. I swear it."

She shook her head gently, her expression a bittersweet mixture of love and acceptance. "No, Edward. My choice saved you... and Silas. The curse would have taken both of you if I hadn't offered myself."

Silas's voice cracked as he whispered, "But there has to be another way..."

Clara's ghostly smile was tender yet resolute. "Sometimes... love is the only thing strong enough to break a curse. My sacrifice wasn't just for you—it was for all who come after us."

Edward's voice trembled violently. "I can't leave you here."

Her gaze softened. "You have to. Live, Edward. Remember me. Tell our story."

Thomas's voice, distant and mournful, echoed through the chamber once more. "The house will always demand a price. But sometimes, love is the only thing stronger than death."

As Clara's spirit began to fade, her final whisper lingered in the stillness: "I'll always be here... beneath these branches."

Edward, tears flowing freely, turned to Silas, his voice a ragged whisper. "We have to leave."

Silas nodded solemnly, the weight of their loss evident in his eyes. "But we'll never forget."

As they ascended from the cellar, the ancient house seemed to hold its breath, its hunger momentarily sated. But beneath its weathered floorboards, an unseen whisper stirred, waiting.

The past never truly rests. And neither do the dead.

EPILOGUE

The Darlington estate stood silent, its once-imposing façade weathered by time, its dark windows gazing blankly upon the surrounding woods. The whispers that once echoed through its halls had quieted, but an uneasy stillness lingered, as though the house itself mourned.

Edward Darlington sat beneath the towering oak in the overgrown garden, the wind stirring the leaves above him in a ghostly rustle. A worn journal rested in his hands—Clara's journal. Its pages were filled with memories, sketches, and the delicate scrawl of her deepest thoughts. His fingers traced her handwriting as if by doing so he could bring her back.

"I still hear you," Edward whispered to the wind. "In every creak of the floorboards, in every sigh of the wind through the trees."

Silas Boone, standing a few feet away, lit a cigarette and exhaled slowly. "You know, Darlington, you're going to haunt yourself if you keep this up." His voice, though tinged with its usual sarcasm, held an undertone of genuine concern.

Edward gave a sad smile. "She's worth the haunting."

Silas walked over, his expression uncharacteristically solemn. "We survived, Edward. She made sure of that. Don't waste what she gave us."

"I won't," Edward said, his voice firm despite the sorrow in his eyes. "I'll make sure the world remembers Clara Langston—the woman who loved so fiercely that not even death could silence her."

Silas smirked faintly. "You always did have a flair for the dramatic."

Edward chuckled softly. "She taught me well."

The wind picked up, carrying with it the faintest whisper, barely audible but unmistakable.

"Always..."

Edward closed the journal gently, holding it close to his chest. The house behind him loomed, its secrets buried but never forgotten.

And somewhere beneath those ancient branches, a love story whispered through the leaves, timeless and eternal.

AFTERWORD

As I close the final chapter of *Beneath These Branches: Haunting of Darlington House*, I am overwhelmed with gratitude.

This story has been a labor of love, fear, and fascination — an exploration of how the past lingers and shapes us.

To the readers who embarked on this chilling journey through Darlington House, thank you for embracing its ghosts and its secrets.

May this tale stay with you, much like a whisper in the night, reminding you that some histories refuse to be forgotten. — Kimberly St. Clair

ACKNOWLEDGEMENT

This novel would not have been possible without the unwavering support of many individuals.

To my family and friends, who encouraged me through countless late nights and haunted imaginings, thank you for believing in this story.

To my editor, whose keen eye and insightful feedback brought out the best in these pages.

To the historians and archivists who fueled my research, and to every reader who cherishes a well-told ghost story — this book is for you.

My deepest gratitude to all who walked beside me through the shadows. — Kimberly St. Clair

ABOUT THE AUTHOR

Kimberly St. Clair

Kimberly St. Clair is a writer with a passion for historical fiction, particularly stories that explore the lives of early settlers and the incredible resilience required to survive in a harsh and unforgiving world. Through her writing, Kimberly seeks to bring the past to life, weaving together the struggles, triumphs, and emotions of those who shaped the landscape we know today.

With a deep love for storytelling, Kimberly writes with the belief that every individual's journey—no matter how small or difficult—is worth telling. Her work is inspired by the untold stories of survival, love, and the unyielding human spirit.

When she's not writing, Kimberly enjoys immersing herself in history, connecting with nature, and exploring the complexities of human relationships. She believes that literature can build bridges between people, offering connection and understanding through the written word.

For now, Kimberly prefers to keep her personal life private, focusing instead on the stories she brings to the world. She hopes that her readers find as much inspiration and strength in these tales as she has in writing them.